FLIGHT OF THE
BLACK SWAN

By J.M. Erickson

Flight of the Black Swan is an action/adventure novella from the *Birds of Flight* series

Flight of the Black Swan
All rights Reserved
Copyright 2015 J. M. Erickson
http://www.jmericksonindiewriter.com

Edited: Suzanne M. Owen
Cover design: Cathy Helms, Avalon Graphics, LLC
http://www.avalongraphics.org

Publisher: J. M. Erickson
http://www.jmericksonindiewriter.net

ISBN: 978-1-942708-03-2 (Soft Cover)
ISBN: 978-1-942708-04-9 (MOBI Format)
ISBN: 978-1-942708-05-6 (ePub Format)

Library of Congress Control Number: 2015902507

Other ebooks by this author:

Action/Adventure Thrillers

Albatross: Birds of Flight - Book One (Revised)
Raven: Birds of Flight - Book Two
Eagle: Birds of Flight - Book Three
Falcon: Birds of Flight – Book Four

Action/Adventure Science Fiction

Future Prometheus I: Emergence & Evolution - Novella I & II
Future Prometheus II: Revolution, Successions & Resurrections - Novellas III, IV & V
Intelligent Design: Revelations

Black Swan

They say you were inevitable
An unknown to be feared,
A force described as formidable
Upon reflection it was clear

A black swan among the white few
The one beauty a sole outlier
Flammes sombres et le feu
Amidst the snow a fire

From the chaos you give order
While in the darkness light
Where reason and love borders
You draw your strength for flight

To those who understand and stay
The rest see as unexpected,
Tu es mon vigueur tout au long de la journée
Black swans, we two, are wedded

Owl: Philadelphia, Pennsylvania USA
May 2nd – 12:30 AM

"'God save thee, ancient Mariner!
From the fiends, that plague thee thus!—
Why look'st thou so?'—With my cross-bow
I shot the ALBATROSS."

> *The Rime of the Ancient Mariner, Part I,* Samuel Taylor
> Coleridge

"I HATE IT WHEN I'm right," John Helms said. With the exception of twelve other passengers traveling in the "quiet cars," he was talking to himself again. He didn't worry too much about talking to himself. He found that when he spoke aloud, it helped organize his thoughts. He looked at his expensive watch and calculated that he would be in Washington, D.C. by 7:30 AM, which would give him more than enough time to get a cup of coffee and meet up with Diane Welch at their appointed time. He looked back out the window to see more of his reflection than anything outside. Of all the passengers, he was decidedly better dressed, well -groomed and clearly prepared for some serious business meeting. If any of the riders were awake, they would have assumed that he was either part of the new security team now dispatched on Acela Express or some type of well -paid law -enforcement specialist or an unfortunate executive whose Learjet was grounded. His clothes, while business formal, were well -tailored, while his solid frame belied an athletic body for a man in his late fifties. The thought of missing his morning run did bother him. He smiled; the weights he lifted made up for that missed opportunity. He looked back at his watch again in the hopes that an hour had passed.

"Hmm...three minutes." He looked back out the window and thought about his destination.

If all went well, he would finally be able to talk to Rachael Janeson directly after nearly three years of her being off the map. He changed his gaze from the darkened window back to his table of multicolored files, all varying in the amount of wear at the edges. After another minute of searching, he found the relatively thin, pink file labeled "Black Swan." Similar to many of the other files, it had multiple surveillance pictures and long-distance telephoto shots, but unlike many of them, nearly all the pictures were obscured, faded, dark and overall it was not easy to see the figures' faces. The borders of each picture and image said either "thought to be Black Swan" or "suspected image of Wolf." After he finished looking at them for the thousandth time, he took out a forty-five -page report generated by his company's Behavioral Risk Assessment Team or BRAT as they preferred to be called. He was very proud of this team of former FBI behavior analysis specialists, psychologists and former criminals - turned -law -enforcement. It was his idea and with Welch's support to create the team, it was a great move. The team was under the watchful eyes of Jill Davis and Denise Cratty. Their management styles complimented each other.

"It's like they're married," he mumbled. He couldn't help but smile as a series of old television shows about odd couples living and working together came immediately to mind. It took effort to shift back to the report. Like so many reports before, their assessments were eerily accurate. Even Gilmore and Johnson from the FBI Regional Office in Boston would send their assessments to his team just for an outside opinion. They always found something new, and what was found was always important. Flipping to the last two pages, Helms started with the highlighted bullet summary of "Projections." He was glad his suspicious nature and obsessiveness with preparing for the disaster was triggered last month when he got his team to work on a detailed projective analysis on what May 2nd would be like this year with the variables of Alexander Burns,

Janeson, her uncle, Regina Panelli, Alica Wise and Jeffery Glenn still unaccounted for for the last three months. Janeson, Wise and Panelli were off-grid entirely while Burns was spotted in Paris and Glenn in Montreal. With Davis and Cratty already keeping an eye on Burns and Dillon and Ramsey scouring the city of Montreal, he still kept wondering why Janeson had not contacted him directly about meeting. The request came through the Russian Embassy directly to Diane Welch. That request to meet came in four days ago. Just as his behavioral team predicted. Helms jumped down to the last paragraph he had read multiple times.

Based on Rachael Margarita Janeson's choice of literature, art, music and past history, she is your classic romantic that is best understood in its classical sense of "Sturm und Drang" or "storm and stress" where extreme emotions are allowed to be expressed as a reaction to logical and rational restrictiveness. Since she has a very deep emotional attachment to Alexander Joshua Burns as a result of near -constant communication for several months prior to his capture by Eric Icarus Daniels, she is prone to sentimental dates, circumstances and passions. This is counterbalanced with her near - photographic memory and recall of key security protocols, top secret operations predating her disappearance, logistical training and prior extensive field work in surveillance, counterinsurgency and counter terrorism. This combination makes for a very compelling and potentially very dangerous scenario, should she be motivated to act. This combination of personal and skill-based competencies were also present when Mr. Burns initiated all his operations against the former Foreign Intelligence Agency and the FBI several years ago on May 2nd . With that very date approaching, and the recent uptick in activities in all of the intelligence communities in Italy, France, UK and Canada, followed by a corresponding decrease in all intelligence chatter in Russia, it is highly likely that a series of events will occur that will put Ms. Janeson and Mr. Burns on the grid again. And in keeping with past histories and analysis, these events will be coordinated and spectacular. Ms. Janeson's familial relationship with Dr. Volkov Volkonoff will make resourcing such a series simple, and Mr. Burns's capacity for facilitating such a highly resourced, well -thought -out plan will be relatively easy. Best course of action is to accept any outreach Ms. Janeson or a designee makes while ensuring that all law enforcement securities are on heightened alert, especially in the Merrimack Valley, Massachusetts, USA. Further, locating Mr. Burns and Ms. Janeson will be critical to circumvent any operations. Locating Dr. Volkonoff will be moot as he is seldom directly connected to any operation when it is in play. In fact, should Dr. Volkonoff be easily located, it is more likely part of the plan and a means of containing variables that might negatively affect a covert operation.

"'Variables that might negatively affect a covert operation.' Like me and Welch. Are you really coming to see us, Rachael? "

Helms put the document back down and looked out the dark window. Periodic flashes of lights and shadows blurred by as he thought about the day to come. He could have taken a journey by plane that would have been three hours but the train's rhythm helped him think, and the seven-hour travel time gave him time.

"How did I miss this?"

Albatross: North Reading, Massachusetts, USA
May 2nd – 8:00 AM

"A speck, a mist, a shape, I wist!
And still it neared and neared:
As if it dodged a water sprite,
It plunged and tacked and veered."

> *The Rime of the Ancient Mariner, Part III,* Samuel Taylor Coleridge

LIEUTENANT STEVE ANDERSEN'S CAR was moving faster than the posted speed. He was in a hurry. He was always anxious every May 2nd even though many Mays had gone by and nothing happened. There were other dates that were also anxiety -provoking but it was the May 2nd anniversary that always got him prickly. Twenty-two minutes ago, he was having a cup of coffee and a hundred -calorie yogurt when his smartphone vibrated and a picture of a well -dressed woman bound to a chair displayed. She was either sleeping, dead or drugged. Disturbing still was that it was Regina Panelli who was supposed to be somewhere unknown in Italy. But the icing on the cake had little to do with her and the date but rather the location. The placement of the chair in the front room was pulled deep from his memory. The unique windows and molding were something he remembered from the gated community in Leverett Circle. Back on May 2nd so many years ago, it was the only completed structure in the development. That's where they found two of Panelli's men who were dead, a dead FIA agent, two wounded FBI agents, and a blind material witness, Samuel Coleridge, or better known as David Caulfield.

"Where it all began," he mumbled.

"What you say, Boss," Officer Dempsey asked. Dempsey was nearly finished with his jelly donut and napkins were all over the place. Since Andersen's car was an old Crown Victoria, he didn't mind. He just hoped that Dempsey didn't get his jelly -stained hands and powdered sugar all over his suit. The consulting job with Welch and Helms was paying for his kids' college and Laura insisted that he dress better for both image and the future.

"Nothing," Andersen said. He pulled the voice -activated police transceiver from the oversized coffee holder and depressed the button to speak. Finding no pushbutton, he remembered that it was voice -activated, with no need to push to talk.

"What's the situation at the site?"

It took just a moment for a female voice to come through clearly.

"I've got eyes and shooters on every exit. There's no movement in or around the property. All the neighbors have been cleared out quietly and there's been no movement in the entire cul-de-sac. The good news is that no cars are in the driveway and the neighbors say the family works and goes to school. There's probably only the woman and anyone inside. How close are you?"

"Five minutes. You got everything done in record time, Jenkins. Good work!"

"Thank you, LT," the voice said. Andersen put the transceiver back in the coffee holder and drove. He felt as if he were being scrutinized by his silent passenger. Even his loud chewing sounds and finger -licking noises were absent, indicating that something was wrong.

"Is there a problem, Dempsey?" Andersen asked. He took his eyes off the road for a moment to see if Dempsey had a heart attack or something. Dempsey's grip on the last quarter of his donut was evidence of life along with what looked like a cross between a scowl and a pout.

"Oh, nothing, boss. I just was wondering why you deployed Jenkins to the crime scene in the first wave, and the new guy as back up, and I'm with you. Just kind of wondering."

Andersen looked back at Dempsey. He was surprised and annoyed that Dempsey had pieced together his lack of competence and the need to put the better-skilled officers on the ground as soon as possible, regardless of rank and length of time in.

"Are we really going to do this?"

"Oh, it's okay. I was just trying to figure it out."

As the silence dragged on, Andersen decided that in celebration for May 2nd, he would try some deception to get Dempsey out of his funk. For better or for worse, the deception he experienced on May 2nd by Dr. David Caulfield was as instructive as it was infuriating.

"How close are you to retirement?" Andersen asked him.

"Ah...about nine years, I think."

"I'll be done in about three. We're kind of close to retirement and I was just trying to make sure that you and I don't take any more risks than we have to. These newer guys have to make their bones. We're all set. We got to train these young kids," Andersen said. For a moment, he almost believed it. He wondered if that was how Caulfield felt when he was giving him his story to keep him out of the game. It took him just a second to remember that David was actually telling him the truth all along except for one small part in the end. Andersen was still thinking of his interview in *Room 8* when he crested the hill and saw the Leverett Circle cul-de-sac of completed, beautiful homes. The house he wanted was the one on the opposite side of the road that he was taking. It looked smaller as a result of his perspective and the fact that there were other houses in the area, as opposed to the last time he surrounded this house when there was just the one.

"So we could hang out, maybe go fishing?" Andersen heard Dempsey say.

"What? I got distracted. What?"

"I said that maybe when we retire, we can hang out together," Dempsey said. Andersen turned to confirm that Dempsey was smiling and seemed happy. Andersen felt his face freeze. Part of his retirement dream was to work with his friends Diane Welch and

John Helms. Next to that, he was looking forward to getting away from some of his coworkers. Dempsey was the top guy on that short list of people he wanted to say goodbye to and mean it. Forever.

"Sure," Andersen said with little emotion and less enthusiasm.

"Cool beans," he heard Dempsey say with a happy tone. Next came the final slurps and chews of the mauled donut corner.

"No act of kindness will go unpunished, "he muttered. He was glad to be waved on through the fence and happy to see that his officers and the SWAT team were all prepared for the tactical assault. Well out of sight of the house, the scene commander and SWAT team leader agreed that the strike force would foot it in from the neighbor's home and take the house from all three entrances at the same time. Andersen popped his trunk and pulled out his vest and started to strap in on.

"Hey boss? Why don't you let the other guys do it? I mean, they have to make their bones," Dempsey said with a confused look on his face.

"I gotta show the leadership thing and I got SWAT and the young lions here going in first. I'm pretty sure I'll reach retirement." Andersen was surprised how quickly he kept up the facade and how easily Dempsey accepted the reasoning. With vest in place, sidearm and ammunition strapped on, Andersen took out his assault rifle. Ever since May 2nd and his skirmish in Boston City Hall, he had taken to having large-caliber weapons with many rounds available whenever possible. Before he checked in with the scene commander, he looked at his text messages from Welch and Dillon to see if they gave any response to the picture he sent of Regina Panelli. There were two.

"Shit. This will piss off her bro. Gotta run. Ramsey thinks she saw Snowflake near McGill. She's carrying two .45 caliber semis. Be careful!"

Andersen shook his head at the thought of Ramsey carrying two semiautomatic hand-guns having high volume and large stopping power.

"Smart girl," he said as he flipped to Welch's text.

"Should have seen that coming. We'll be in place soon to see if Black Swan actually shows. I hate May 2nd! Be careful! Laura will be pissed and I don't want to deal with your sister!"

"Yeah, that would be bad."

Andersen made it to the Beta Group just as the last piece of instructions and placements was being arranged. As expected, he was placed near the rear. After five more minutes of review, they were off running across well-kept lawns, sprinkler systems, fences and lawn furniture recently put out.

After just a few minutes, Andersen was back to the house where it all began years ago. Following his cues and stacking up, he watched the Beta Leader motion the rammers up to take the door out. Andersen shifted to give them room. The leader gave the signal to take the door on three. He watched the fingers count down. After nearly three decades of police work, forced entries still made him sweat.

The door was down on three and the team moved in with lightening speed. Andersen heard the team from the front door and the basement sweep in. The kitchen area, hallway and front room looked so different than the last time: more cramped and tight with furniture and appliances making moving tighter and more difficult. It took less than sixty seconds for a series of "all clears" to indicate that there were no armed assailants in the home waiting for them. Just to make sure they weren't sitting on an explosive trap, the two guys ahead of Andersen were a demolition expert and a bomb specialist. Another minute after the all-clear, the bomb experts pronounced the house bomb-free. All the while Andersen stood over a heavily sedated Regina Panelli, well-dressed as always with her hair still in place. The room she sat in was a well-appointed formal parlor devoid of children's toys. Its cleanliness and perfect arrangement made the bound woman and the lined piece of white paper lying on the floor in front of her stand out even more. All the words looked different except for one: *Volk*. That looked more like a name than just a word. The three words were easy but the rest looked very different. With the heavy footsteps of officers slowing down, sirens and more men and women came flooding in. Andersen took out his smart phone, found his camera application and took a picture. Twenty seconds later, he had the language and the meaning.

"Russian? Shit."

Chernyy lebed' letit. Volk stebli . The Black Swan flies. The Wolf stalks.

Andersen lost track of how long he had been looking at the phrase before he sent it to Welch. He was about to send it to Dillon when Dempsey arrived.

"You okay, Boss?" Andersen looked up to see there was concern in his face.

"Yeah. Why?"

"You look pretty white, Boss. Like you saw a ghost or something." Andersen looked around at the same room that years ago on the same day he met a dead Agent Maxwell, a live David Caulfield pretending to be a dead writer, and a very dangerous former agent who had a family he would protect at all cost.

"I kind of did," Andersen muttered as he forwarded the same note to Dillon and Welch.

Black Swan: Washington, D.C., USA
May 2nd – 8:30 AM

"With throats unslaked, with black lips baked,
We could not laugh nor wail;
Through utter drought all dumb we stood!
I bit my arm, I sucked the blood,
And cried, A sail! a sail!"

> *The Rime of the Ancient Mariner, Part III,* Samuel Taylor Coleridge

"IT DOESN'T GET MUCH prettier than this. This place never gets old," Diane Welch said to her peer and colleague John Helms. Even though the cherry blossoms were beyond peak, the sights and scents only enhanced the Lincoln Memorial Reflecting Pool's awe-inspiring view of Washington D.C.'s national treasures. It had taken years and millions to repair the monument and clean up the algae but from Welch's perspective, it was all worth it.

"You'd think that it would get old but it still inspires me," Helms said. His imposing size, buzz cut and hands planted firmly on the hips certainly screamed military even though his tailored suit cried Wall Street. She looked down at her own attire and smiled. Her stance was classic for a Marine: feet a shoulder width apart, shoulders squared and her hands held behind her back. Her suit was light olive green linen and paired with practical shoes should the need arise. The simple cut and classic design of her attire was similar to Helms's, save for the brown color and perfectly matched amber tie on a starched, white shirt. Welch couldn't help but chuckle when she looked at both of them together.

"What's so funny?"

"Look at us, John. We look like we just walked out of the Marine recruiting office and changed into the same civilian clothes. How the hell does this happen?"

Helms looked at her and then looked down at himself. He nodded and looked back over the reflecting pool.

"We Marines are simple folk. We may get lucky and make some money, if we live, but our tastes are pretty straightforward and simple."

Welch narrowed her eyes and returned to look at the same site. Helms had been far more cryptic and quiet the last several days. Getting a text from a secured source, the Russian Embassy, that his former mentee, Rachael Janeson, wanted to meet with them, was something that was obviously weighing on him. Welch liked Janeson and was impressed with her intelligence, skills and beauty as well as her social awkwardness. While she had worked with her for a couple of years, Helms had groomed her from a recruit to eventually take his place as director at Boston's FBI Regional office. Her defection from the service following the constant harassment by the NSA was understandable to Welch but not so much to Helms. Worse, both of them saw her changing, mutating, evolving into her own objectives long before the NSA began its intense background check. In fact, both of them pinpointed the exact time and circumstance of her metamorphosis. Alexander Burns. It all started with him and his dog. And the NSA discoveries, a source of embarrassment more than security issues, simply put fire to gasoline.

"You've been pretty quiet and reflective these last couple of days," Welch said. She watched him to see if he would do his usual thing when he was upset. After years of working with him daily, it was easy to figure out his tells. As expected, Helms sighed first, tensed his jaw then released it followed by clenching and unclenching of his fists. The fact that he did all three in that order indicated he was either stressed, angry or both. The rolling of his shoulders looked like it might be another indicator. She made note to watch for it in the future.

"It doesn't make sense, Janeson wanting to come in. And the fact that we find Regina Panelli at Leverett Circle on May 2nd, where and when it all started, gets me nervous."

"Yeah. It doesn't sit well with me at all."

"And last I checked, Janeson was still abroad, somewhere. Burns was last seen in Austria but appears in Paris, and somehow Panelli finds her way from Italy back to North Reading, tied up like a present."

"Or maybe a peace offering," Welch said as she looked back down at an open video file. It showed a well-dressed woman who appeared to be sleeping though she was bound in a chair. The video came in at 7:35 AM from an unknown IP address. She was able to forward it immediately to Andersen and then to Gilmore and Johnson at the Bureau in Boston. In less than five minutes, Andersen had a location and was en route, and the Bureau had a lead on Angelo Panelli in Newport, Rhode Island. With these events happening in Merrimack Valley, and it being May 2nd, Andersen and the Bureau mobilized all resources as if they were preparing for another Gulf War. Specialist Martin and his elite team were also dispatched to detain Regina's better half, Angelo. Welch was feeling as if she was missing all the action. Just like last time. Just as Burns had planned it so many years ago. She pulled back to the present as she remembered her question about whether it was all about a truce.

"Peace offering? Maybe. But I think she would have simply called me and not have gone through all of this. This looks more like Burns and the resources of his old Foreign Intelligence Agency which, last I recall, we all disassembled. No. There's a series of events going down all at the same time."

"Just like BRAT predicted."

"Yup. Have you heard from Littleton, by the way?"

"No. Murphy's gone off-grid too," Welch said. Her phone vibrated to indicate that two texts came in.

The first message came in with an image of the same woman but there was a handwritten note on lined paper she immediately recognized as Russian. She read the note and the translation underneath.

Chernyy lebed' letit. Volk stebli The black swan flies. The Wolf stalks.

"Oh hell," she said.

"What's wrong?"

"I'll tell you in a minute. Let me get the next one first."

She keyed it up and the message was a short one from Thomas "Nine" Williams at her three o'clock.

Lone figure, well-dressed, coming in from 3 o'clock. Looks unarmed and no backup. Not our lady but may be more impressive. Definitely not here for the view.

Welch re-read the text again to make sure she got it right. From her vantage point, she could see the figure solely as a result of Nine's warning. The groups of casually dressed tourists and families made the well-dressed lone man stand out. The Park Rangers were also doing a good job redirecting these groups away from their general area. She saw the closest rangers talking into their transceivers. It was obvious they were letting the man come through to them unhindered. She was about to tell Helms but he was already looking beyond her at the man approaching. She waited to tell him, wondering if his eyesight was better than hers.

"I'll be damned. I hate it when I'm right," Helms said.

"Who is it?"

"The 'Wolf.' And he's in sheep's clothing too."

"That makes sense," Welch said. "The note at Regina's foot was Russian. It read the 'black swan flies. The Wolf stalks.'"

Welch felt Helms looking at her and then he looked back.

"I really do hate it when I'm right."

"How can you see that far? Contacts?" Welch asked.

"Nope. Good genes. Exercise too."

"I exercise and my eyes are like shit."

"You spent too much time in Pakistan and Afghanistan. Too much field work. Too much sun. And doing elliptical and weights on the machine are not the same as running on pavement and free weights."

Welch nodded and looked in the same direction at the man. At a distance, from the dwindling clumps of people, it was easy to see he was slightly shorter than the average man, maybe five foot six . But what he lacked in height he possessed in breadth, and even from afar it was easy to see that he was not fat but rather broad and muscular. His dossier pictures and images didn't do him justice, though there were not many of them. His files were thick and page after page was mostly riddled with his "alleged involvement" or "orchestration" and "presumed connection". The only thing concrete was that he was a medical doctor by training and a close friend of the Russian President and his family. At the same time, his familiarity with all things covert and top-secret was legendary. Fiercely loyal to his friends and family and often working alone, he was dubbed "Wolf." Up until recently, his connection to Mr. and Mrs. Janeson was unknown much to the embarrassment of the US government. His niece, known as the "Black Swan," was not a fugitive or an enemy combatant but a walking command and control center with a wealth of black ops and military secrets all neatly organized and collated in her head.

"I do hate it when you're right. Things just got complicated."

"About the exercise? I'm right about that for sure," Helms said.

"No, John. About everything going to shit today. I'm beginning to hate May."

"Yup. Well, at least we get a chance to gather some intel," he said.

"Maybe." Welch and Helms waited until Dr. Volkov Volkonoff was close enough to begin their tête-a-tête. Welch waited patiently. By Helm's clenching jaw, she was pretty sure he was not as patient. She noticed he rolled his shoulders. There was no pattern. A minute or two passed and Dr. Volkonoff was now right beside them, all three now standing next to the reflecting pool.

"Mrs. Welch. Mr. Helms," he said in English though it was heavily accented.

""Dr. Volkonoff," Welch said for the two of them. She took a good look at him before he turned to look at the reflecting pool and the monuments just beyond. He stood akimbo. His hair was nearly completely black with only a few strands of gray hair indicating he might be older than fifty. His face was pleasant and he seemed prone to smiling, while his hair was a little too long and wiry. But it was his piercing blue eyes, shape of his nose and jaw line, and pale skin that transmitted that he was closely related to Rachael Janeson. His suit was far more expensive than theirs combined. His shoes, matching vest and watch chain gave him an imperious look. His disposition and demeanor ran contrary to his clothes. The man known as the 'Wolf' seemed disarming, low-key, and warm.

"My sister tells me often that Rachael is very much like me when I was young," he said as he continued looking out over the pool. Welch was not sure what to say. Fortunately Helms fielded the question.

"So, do we need to thank you for finding Regina Panelli for us?"

"Yes and no. Rachael triangulated her possible locations and Mr. Burns did reconnaissance. I was only involved in transportation and delivery. A small task, really."

"And the location of her brother?"

"Rachael. Mr. Burns and Rachael had Mr. Jeffery Glenn in the UK several months ago and Ms. Ramsey and Ms. Dillon almost had him but his skills at evasion are impressive, especially when the Mossad is assisting him," Dr. Volkonoff said. He took out his pocket watch and then went on talking.

"Maybe they will have better luck in Montreal. They had more time but they still have to narrow the field and get local law enforcement to cover a larger area."

Shit! Where is he getting his intel?

"And why are you doing this?" Helms asked.

"I'm not doing anything. I'm just pick-up and delivery. Rachael and Mr. Burns are doing the logistics, reconnaissance and organizing. I'm not supposed to be here. I just wanted to talk to you both to ask a favor," he said in a lower voice.

Welch and Helms exchanged looks. There were very few

tourists and families in the area. Welch was grateful for that. The Park Rangers were doing a good job keeping people out of their general area. Dr. Volkonoff turned to face them both. There was an avuncular look of concern on his face as he spoke.

"My sister, brother-in-law and I would appreciate it very much if you were to let Rachael and Mr. Burns contact you rather than you looking for them. While I appreciate Mr. Tombs's effort on behalf of your President to keep the NSA and CIA off of my niece's back, I think you two will have more influence."

A silence fell around them. There was a slight warm breeze that created a small ripple on the pool.

"We work for a private consulting firm for the Department of Defense," Welch started. She was surprised how quickly Dr. Volkonoff responded with shaking his head and putting his hands back on his hips.

"No, no, no, Mrs. Diane Welch, Marine Warrant Officer. Your steady rise and sudden resignation from the service, facilitated by your commanding officer at the time, Mr. John Helms, was only the beginning of an illustrious if not wanted career. Mr. Robert Tombs's recruitment to have you and your hand-selected team lead and operate Allied Federation International, Incorporated was a stroke of ingenuity for someone allegedly devoid of creativity." The doctor's faint smile conveyed the irony. For the first time since their meeting, Welch felt herself relax just a moment. She saw Helms trying to keep the corners of his mouth from inching upwards.

"Well, Mr. Tombs is better known for his consistency, going by the book, and no surprises," Welch finally said.

"Yes. Well to my point; you and I know that Rachael's social skills are at best limited. She has benefited greatly from Mr. Johnson's and Mr. Gilmore's hands-on assistance over the years, and Mr. Martin's assistance in helping her act, an exceptional piece of work, I must say. "

"You know a lot about the people in her world," Helms said.

Dr. Volkonoff smiled. Welch was surprised how warm his eyes looked. His eyes shimmered like the sun rays on the reflecting pool.

"Yes. I especially appreciate your stepping up several times to be her patron. You were her uncle when I could not be there. For that I personally thank you." Welch felt her eyes widen. She turned to see her large Marine colleague flush with red. His silence spoke volumes. Welch took the lead to carry on the discussion to give Helms a chance to recover.

"Let's say we did. Let's say we stepped in. What can I offer the NSA and CIA to stay off of her back? I've tried logic, reason and influence and got nowhere."

"That is easy. Rachael and Mr. Burns seem determined to focus on tying up loose ends from the Eric Icarus Daniels era as well as some other geopolitical issues that run contrary to their sense of justice. I would tell your NSA and CIA that you struck a deal with 'the Wolf' and that they work for me. By working for me and by our meeting, we now have an alliance. Collaboration is very likely between our governments as a result of their loyalty to you and me. But if they are detained, arrested, or harassed, I will take that as an affront, as will my President and cabinet. That would be very stressful for everyone." A tense moment materialized out of thin air. The beautiful Washington D.C. Monument seemed distant, dark and far away as images of Russian tanks rolling into Belarus, Moldova, Finland, Poland and all the others in the middle of a torrential rainstorm flooded Welch's mind.

"You mean NATO, Crimea and Ukraine stressful?" Helms said.

"Worse. One is politics, for flag and country. This would be personal. It is family."

The subtle change in expression, tone and presentation gave credence and meaning to his code name of Wolf. His pale skin seemed to darken and his deep blue eyes pierced through her as his body remained still. The warm breeze with its floral scent did not seem to fit with the Wolf. Suddenly, the kind, gentle doctor returned as smoothly as he had disappeared. Welch felt the sun but she was wet, not by rain but sweat. She was glad to be back in the present.

"So please do your best to express my wishes to the powers that be," he said. He smiled again and started to walk away in the other direction. Welch exchanged another look with Helms who looked as surprised as she. Welch was about to ask a question when Dr. Volkonoff stopped short as if he remembered something and turned around with questions of his own.

"By the way, why is Sergeant Thomas Williams's code name 'Nine'?"

Welch felt a little better. There was a question she could answer.

"A famous Boston Red Sox baseball player. The name was Ted Williams and his number was the number nine. I'm guessing his parents were part of Red Sox Nation back in the day, before there was a nation." Welch furrowed her brows at her explanation. It was clearly American, specifically Boston.

The doctor looked confused. If he was still unclear, he decided to move to his next question.

"Why does your intelligence community refer to my niece as the 'Black Swan'?"

Welch narrowed her eyes. She didn't have an answer for that. She was surprised when Helms immediately answered the question.

"It's a probability and statistics term used in finances. It's an event, circumstance or occurrence that is unexpected and comes as a surprise even though we should have seen it coming. Something unpredictable that can be figured out, post facto. I guess it made sense." Welch found herself looking at Helms first and then back at Dr. Volkonoff. He shook his head as if he clearly understood.

"Yes. That does make sense," he said. With that, he turned back around and continued walking just like many of the other tourists further away. The Park Rangers gave Welch a look to see if the coast was clear. She nodded and took out her phone. Helms was already on his, texting away.

"You texting Ramsey and Dillon," Welch said more than asked. She already secured an early text from Davis and was getting her thoughts in order. The time in France had to be close to three in the afternoon. If all was well, Davis, Cratty, French Secret Service and INTERPOL had Burns adequately covered. The fact that the doctor mentioned that maybe Ramsey and Dillon might be lucky catching Glenn in Montreal, a lead she thought was known only to them, indicated that everything was up for grabs.

"What a day. He knows way more than I like," Welch said.

"Yup. He wasn't what I expected," Helms said as he walked and texted at the same time. Welch was following suit.

"Speaking of unexpected, how the hell did you know what 'black swan' meant?"

"We marines are not just pretty faces and all muscle. We got intelligence. Oorah?"

"Oorah" Welch said. A couple more sentences and she would hit "Send". A nagging thought kept bothering her about Littleton and Murphy being off-grid.

Whenever that happens, shit is about to fly.

Another gentle breeze with a cherry-blossom scent filled her senses. If it wasn't for all the questions, it would have been nice to enjoy the environment.

Raven: Newport, Rhode Island, USA
May 2nd – 8:45 AM

"Are those her ribs through which the sun
Did peer, as through a grate?
And is that woman all her crew?
Is that a Death? and are there two?
Is Death that woman's mate?"

> *The Rime of the Ancient Mariner, Part III,* Samuel Taylor Coleridge

"ALL I'M SAYING IS that Rosemarie looks up to you, Becky. And I think you're getting a little too thin," John Murphy said into her earpiece. Becky found herself only partially listening. The Newport Mansion commonly known as the *Breakers* in Newport, Rhode Island, certainly lived up to its grandeur and opulence that one would expect of the Vanderbilts. Close to the North Atlantic and not far from the other mansions along Ochre Point Avenue, Becky took a moment just to take in the last part of her private tour and really look at the mahogany staircase and glistening chandeliers.

"I wish I got here when we all lived here," she said. "David would have loved this."

"Dr. Caulfield sounds like my kind of guy. Smart, articulate and really knows his local history. Did you know how the *Breakers* got its name?"

Becky took a deep sigh and shifted back into mission mode. Her lack of response to Murphy's rhetorical questions always meant he should start out at the earliest of historical dates of wherever she was and bring her up to the present without leaving out any detail, no matter how trivial it might be. When she was covering him for hours many years ago in Providence to discourage the Panelli family from messing with her, Murphy and her girls, she had to listen to him for hours. Based on the raw intelligence she got from Burns and his sources, she would only have to deal with Murphy's lecture for a few more minutes. With the private viewers now on their way and the tour guides off to round up the next private, select group, Becky's sharp exit to the rear of the home was easy. The mansion's floor plan was easy to get and committing it to memory was easy with four days' preparation. Dressed in dark slacks, white blouse and dark blazer, she was sure she looked like the other tour guides, though her dark earpiece did depart from their ensemble. Still, the wire was well placed behind her ear and it blended in with her short, black hair. Her hair was too black. She had overshot her goal of brown by several shades. Years of criticizing Samantha for dyeing her own hair seemed to haunt her often. She stopped once she got to the massive servants' kitchen and tried once again to tighten her belt. It was too big on her. She pulled it off and put it on the counter. She was also swimming in her blouse and blazer. It fit very well about a month ago. Things change.

"I hate it when he's right," she said to herself.

"When who's right?" Murphy cut in. Becky was very surprised that he heard her at all, but then she remembered his saying that he couldn't remember something and there was a pause.

"I might have lost a little bit too much weight."

"You think? Not that it's any of my business."

"And it's not," Becky said. Murphy was undeterred when others would have just backed away.

"I'm just saying you start losing weight every year at this time like clockwork and you never gain it back. You keep doing this and we'll have to put you in the hospital. Do you even have your period anymore?"

Becky's smooth movements to the back door that opened up onto a spacious veranda were halted.

"Murphy! For Christ's sake! We got a job to do. Can you back off the questions? And it's none of your business if I have my period. Jesus, Murphy."

"I'm just saying that after you lose so much weight, you lose your period."

"Murphy – just stop and focus. I'm about to go out to see our target," she said. Even as she spoke succinctly, she looked up the media folders and found a short repeating video of a well-dressed woman who looked sound asleep bound in a chair.

"Is the team in place?"

"You mean your all-female crazy team? They sure are. I'm glad we had a couple of days to set this up. Any word on how Burns's contact got Angie's itinerary? I mean, I wish I had that kind of intel back in the day."

"I don't ask and he doesn't tell. You got your guys covering the drive and a containment team in case this all goes south?"

"Yes, I got a *containment* team. Where do you get these terms from?"

From her vantage point it was easy to see three guards at the veranda's perimeter and two guards standing right next to Angelo Panelli and his niece. Becky felt some sweat trickling down her neck and armpits. This was the third interaction she had with the Boston North End crime family leader, though it would be the first time they would ever meet face to face. The first time was when the Panellis went looking for her and the girls when they were in witness protection and the other time was not too long after as she shot him and a number of his protection from a balcony. For some reason, seeing and even talking to him made it all real. She also didn't have to do a thing. She could have let Murphy deal with it. But when she heard his niece would be there, she thought her point would be better made by a woman, mother and a person who shot him before.

"You okay, Becky?" Murphy asked. He sounded like the grandfather she imagined she had in an alternate universe, minus the crime. Murphy might have been the former South Boston crime boss twenty years ago, but losing his son, gaining a granddaughter and then another one, had changed him. Her thoughts fluttered to

Samantha and David immediately. Samantha would have thought she was crazy showing up unarmed, while David would have made it clear that she was being reckless. Both would have worried and done everything to keep Emma and Rosemarie safe. That thought strengthened her resolve.

"Fuck it. I'm going in," she said.

"Okay. We got your back. Not to add any pressure, though, but Fitzy tells me that Special Agent Martin and his team are on their way."

"Damn it to all hell! How long?"

"Sixty minutes with this traffic."

"How the hell did Gilmore and Johnson get Martin on the case? Shit." Becky pulled the earphone out of her ear but kept the smartphone on. She held the phone in her hand and waited for it to go dark before she proceeded. She looked back out the door and saw two young women servers each carrying back a tray of empty dishes as Murphy's voice quietly spoke.

"Burns's intelligence is spot on but there is bound to be some kind of leak somewhere. And with the Bureau on the hunt for one of their own, especially on this date, I'm guessing they've been working overtime for the last couple of weeks. Be happy we're here right now."

The servers were just five feet away from the door. Becky looked down and saw that though the phone was on, it looked off.

"Going dark, Murphy. Listen and respond. You'll know the signal to come alive."

"Good luck, Becky. And be careful."

"Will do."

Becky opened the door for the two women. They were pleasantly surprised that someone was there. Becky came out to see them in plain view of the guards and asked a question she already knew the answer to.

"Excuse me. Is there a Mr. Panelli, a Mr. Angelo Panelli here?" she asked the taller of the two.

"Why, yes. He's right over there. You'll have to go see the chief security guy over there first. His name is Gino," she said as she pointed to a very large, dark man who seemed to burst out of his suit.

"Thank you," Becky said. She continued holding the door for them. Once she was sure they were both inside, Becky made a direct though cautious course to Gino. She conjured up her meek, weak demeanor. Because of her tiny frame, she was pretty sure she would come across as non-threatening. As she approached, she felt a series of eyes surveying her. It was clear that this team was taking risk assessment very seriously no matter how hard she tried to look small. Gino met her long before she got close to her target's table. She couldn't help but notice that he walked with a definite limp. Since she had been several stories above her multiple targets that hot day, she was not sure if the limp was her handiwork or something unrelated.

"If you could just remain still for a moment, Miss, and raise your hands up," Gino said. His deep baritone voice was almost as intimidating as his massive hands. Still, she was impressed that his touch, while clearly strong and his search thorough, was gentle. She had her entire body patted down by the giant while at the same time he spoke in a calm fashion. His caring voice and tone almost made her forget that his hands were all over her body. She tried to focus on his questions as a sudden fear of a cavity search flooded her thoughts.

"And what business do you have with Mr. Panelli, Miss?

"It's Becky Littleton, and I have my headphones in my pocket on the right side."

His hands and breathing paused for just a moment before he resumed.

"And your business, Mrs. Littleton?"

Becky paused at the surname "Mrs." It was clear that he knew who she was.

Okay. Here we go.

"Just a quick conversation about the future and a video message from Mr. Alexander Burns about his sister." Her voice shifted from meek and quiet to deadly firm and committed.

"I see." Gino retracted his hands, took two steps back, and waved two men from the table over and produced a large caliber gun in his right hand. While he kept it down and to the side, it was easy to see that shooting her was on the agenda. One man went right behind her and the other leaned in to listen to Gino's whispering. All the while Gino kept his eyes fixed on her. The man that was listening to Gino looked right at him in shock, then at Becky and then back at him.

"For real?" he said.

"As real as a heart attack," Gino calmly said. The man's eyes looked back at her and formed into slits while the corners of his mouth tightened and his ears seemed to pull back as if he were a Doberman Pincher.

"Alright. Follow me, Mrs. *Littleton*," the man said with a sneer. As she fell into step, she also noticed that he too had a limp, though not as pronounced as Gino's.

Nice job, Becky. Talk about a hostile crowd.

The morning sun was warm with a slight shore breeze. The smell of the sea salt and fresh morning dew on the grass hung in the air and birds could be heard chirping in the perfectly trimmed bushes. Becky was impressed with the scene. Still, her homes in Greece and Spain were more to her liking; more organic, real and in the moment, not locked in the past. Instead of feeling fear and anger, Becky was surprised she felt sadness. Her homes with David and Samantha were all gone. She still had Emma and Burns. She now had Rosemarie, and for better or worse, she had Murphy as well. Her thoughts were interrupted by her target's argument on the phone. Murphy had warned her that Angelo's perfect look was only matched by his unusually deep voice and short stature.

"...and when you find out who tipped off Martin and his team, let me know so I can handle them personally," Angelo's deep voice said with a dead calm.

"It was probably Boston Regional FBI team that sent them. They probably got the intel from Alexander Burns," Becky said loudly as she approached the few feet left.

Angelo's eyes snapped up to look right at her and then shifted to the guard.

"Mrs. *Littleton* says she has a message from Alexander Burns," he said with contempt.

Angelo looked right back at her and then spoke into the cell phone.

"I gotta go," he said and closed it. He tossed the cell on his folded napkin, picked up his cup of coffee, sat back in his chair and took a sip. Becky swore she heard some kind of seagull in the distance. She focused back on Angelo who was still sitting back, sipping coffee. A young woman with striking features sat quietly to his right. Her sunken-in, red eyes were evidence to lack of sleep and crying. Becky felt sympathy for her. How many times had she been through that. *Tony. Samantha. David.* The young woman's pale, haggard look was at odds with her elegant dress, manicured nails, perfectly groomed hair with tasteful jewelry. The exterior didn't matter. It was clear to see that the woman looked like shit on the inside.

"So. We finally meet." His voice was deeper than she expected.

"Yes." Becky didn't add anything more. She was very surprised at how calm she felt. Her internal clock was running. She had maybe fifty-five minutes to get her business done before Martin and his team came in with probably the entire Providence police, state troopers and a National Guard regiment.

"So? That's it? 'Yes?' You think you can walk in her here, involve yourself in my business and then just say 'yes'?"

Becky felt her face begin to burn and anger creep up inside at the mention of being involved in his business. Without asking, Becky slowly moved to an empty seat across from Angelo. The young woman was all eyes as Angelo was clearly annoyed at her sitting down as if she were a welcomed guest. With her eyes still locked on his deep brown, recessed eyes, Becky found her words with ease, and placed her smartphone in the middle of the table.

"*I* involved *myself* in *your* business? I don't remember thinking about you when I was in Spain. You know, Angelo? When your people showed up and killed my husband, my friends. I don't ever remember jumping in there to mess with your business when your people came looking for me and my girls when we went off-grid in witness protection. And then when your people shot Alex in the ass, while it was funny, I don't think I thought to mess with your business. But you see, Angelo, the problem is that you messed with my girls. You messed with their grandfather and they love their grandfather. So don't sit there and tell me that I went looking for the shit when you were the asshole that came after me and my family, bitch."

The air was still and the smell of flowers was suddenly strong. Everything seemed to freeze in place. Angelo's visage was dead still. It was only the sniffle from the young woman that broke the silence. With her eyes still focused like lasers on Angelo, Becky softened her voice as she addressed the distressed woman.

"I'm sorry you had to hear that, Veronica. I know how important family is to you. And that's what I wanted to talk to your uncle about."

"How do you know my name?" the young woman blurted out.

"What are you talking about?" Angelo said. His tone and even deeper pitch indicated the true depths of his anger and hatred towards her. Becky pointed to her smartphone. He leaned back towards the table, put his cup down and picked up the phone. His touch on the screen immediately opened the file that had the video of the sleeping, bound woman, his sister Regina. He watched the short image.

"Is that mom?" Veronica asked. Her voice was desperate. Angelo put up his hand to silence her. Tears burst out of her eyes. Becky felt really sad.

"Where is she?"

"She's alive and she's probably going to be in FBI custody soon, I bet," Becky started before Angelo cut her off.

"No. You're going to be my guest until we get this matter settled. It will be an even exchange," he said as he waved Gino over.

"That's what I like about you, Angelo. You value family. Murphy was right about that."

"You're going to wish you had killed me back in Providence if I don't get my sister back," he said. He was standing now with Becky's smartphone in one hand and taking another swig of coffee in his other. Becky remained sitting even as the two guards came up to move her.

"I could have killed you, all of you, but I didn't. I wish I could but when you kill people, it changes you. You end up thinking about stuff. Things that you didn't understand at first become clear. You know? When you read the Bible and it says things that make no sense at first but then the world and life changes you. Hey, Angelo? Have you ever heard of this verse 'For what is a man profited, if he shall gain the whole world, and lose his own soul'?"

Becky was almost certain that Angelo's mouth slackened for just a moment in shock. He had to think that she was crazy. He recovered quickly and shook his head as if to shake off any insanity that might be catching.

"What are you talking about?" His cup was now on the table. Becky smiled.

"You think this is a game?" he continued.

"No Angelo. I'm the Angel of Death. Well, forget about the angel part. Just Death. I couldn't help but notice that you got a stain on your very nice shirt. Is that linen or really good cotton?"

For the first time, her target seemed genuinely annoyed. He picked up his napkin and went to wipe the iridescent red dot on his shirt right over his sternum. He took a long moment to look at it.

"Angie? I've got one too," Veronica said. Her voice was tired but not scared. Becky gave her credit. Angelo looked down at her. He gave her a reassuring smile and then turned back to look at Becky.

"If anything happens to her, you don't leave here alive."

"Me? No. I'm already dead, Angelo. You killed my husband and the government killed my sister. I've been dead for a while. I'm Death."

"You won't hurt anyone?"

Becky closed her eyes for just a moment. It must have looked to Angelo that he had called her bluff. Becky opened her eyes and cleared her voice to speak firmly.

"Target to my left and right."

One second later, the two men on each side of her spun violent forward before they crashed into the elegant table. Becky felt warm liquid—blood—hit each side of her, as the 30-caliber bullets severed major arteries. By the force and the amount of blood, she guessed that the shooters used automatic sniper rifles with silencers to cover the multiple shots. The table was upended and on the ground, dishware scattered all over. Veronica screamed and was enveloped by Angelo's arms protectively. Becky sighed and then felt the muzzle of a gun at the back of her head in addition to the splatters of blood on both sides of her face, blazer and hands. She had to look like some kind of black and red bird.

"Call them off or you'll die," she heard Gino say.

"Gino. I like you. So before you make any sudden moves, you might want to talk to your boss. They still have infrared dots on them," Becky said quietly. There were no sounds with the sole exception of Veronica's muffled whimpering and the sound of a bird above the trees of the estate. It was a very dark bird. A raven.

"Nevermore," Becky muttered, her mind searching for where she had heard the story of a man who lost his wife and was tormented by a raven. *David would have known.*

There was a long pause before Gino spoke again. Becky was pretty sure that Gino saw the dots and probably knew that he would be dead seconds after he pulled the trigger.

"Mr. Panelli? What do you want to do, Sir?" There was still silence. Becky crossed her legs. She was wondering why she was not more frightened than she thought she should be.

Maybe I'm really already dead. Maybe it's for real? I wonder what David would say. Wishful thinking?

"What do you want?" she heard Angelo say.

Without another thought, Becky leaned into the muzzle of the gun, turned and looked down the barrel before she pushed it away from her head. To her own surprise, Gino didn't pull the trigger and he then put the gun in his holster.

"I just want you to forget about me, the girls and Murphy. You want to fight someone? Bobby Fitzpatrick says he's waiting for you."

"And if I don't?" Angelo's eyes were still hot with anger.

Becky looked directly into his eyes. His hot anger shifted to cool as his eyes narrowed as if confused. Her own thoughts came to her tongue before she could catch them.

"I've been dead too long, Angelo, to care. I live for the girls but it's in pain. Kill me, Angelo. I'll see my brother, my sister and my husband," she said as she stood up from her chair. Her voice was something she had not recognized: cold, hollow, empty and despairing. It must have sounded frightening to a person who used fear of death as a threat.

"You don't get it, do you, Angelo? I'm just the messenger. Burns found Regina in Italy. He managed to get her transported to North Reading, Massachusetts. He found out you and Veronica would be here. He located Veronica at Boston College three months ago and her brother Nick at Brown last month. He knows where Joey, Tim and Suzanne are. If I'm dead, I get to rest and see family. If I am killed or the girls hurt or harm comes to Murphy, Veronica, Nick and everyone, they'll disappear first, and pieces will be sent back to you slowly, surely. And once it starts, it won't stop until the whole Panelli, Conti, De Luca, Rizzo, all the families, their families and friends are dead. Angelo. They will all die. Nevermore."

Angelo was silent. Veronica's whimpering stopped and Becky heard Gino's heavy breathing.

"And he will make sure you are last. To witness all this," Becky added before she sat down and crossed her legs. She smoothed out her blood-soaked slacks and looked at her crossed legs for a moment. She had to agree that Murphy was right. Her legs betrayed how thin she was and it was easy to feel all of her ribs. If she lived, she had to start taking her antidepressants again. Becky focused on her present situation. She was surprised Angelo was still quiet.

"So, Angelo, the choice is yours. Live and let live, or End of Days. I'm just the messenger."

Becky was surprised by Angelo's response.

"You're Lady Death."

"No. Just Death."

Snow Owl: Montreal, Quebec, Canada
May 2nd – 9:00 AM

"Her *lips were red,* her *looks were free,*
Her locks were yellow as gold:
Her skin was as white as leprosy,
The nightmare Life-in-Death was she,
Who thicks man's blood with cold."

The Rime of the Ancient Mariner, Part III , Samuel Taylor Coleridge

"FIFTEEN MINUTES, RUTH? I've been ducking them for the last two days. Every time I think I lost them, they show up," Jeffery Glenn said quietly into his wireless earpiece. He was successful in blending in as an eager graduate student from McGill University trying to get early admission into the Redpath Museum. There was a small group of people milling about who looked pretty eager to get into the natural history museum. He searched his pockets for a spare tube of sunscreen lotion for the tenth time in the last hour. He found that same empty tube in his front jacket pocket and squeezed it. It helped him think.

"What do you want from me, Jeffery? John got a fast car but traffic is not our friend here. Avenue du Parc, near the cinema, will be clear for sure," Helen said in her clear English with only a hint of Israeli accent.

"What the hell, Helen? That's four blocks from here in broad daylight. Ramsey and Dillon were a half a block away when I turned in here. And there's bound to be the local police searching for me too!"

"Not really. John has created a series of diversions that pulled the police across town. That said, I assume that since your women friends are still in the area, they must assume it is a distraction and that you might be close. They are as intelligent as they are pretty," Helen said. Glenn rolled his eyes and instinctively touched the scar on his cheek—a war wound from the Torrox, Spain fiasco given to him courtesy of Ana Ramsey, one of many women that wanted him dead.

"You got a thing for Ramsey, don't you? You like them crazy?"

"No. I like passion. These two women have great passion. I do have a preference for darker skin, and birth control would not be an issue but I'm afraid my affiliation with you probably eliminated any chance I might have with Ana." Glenn sighed and closed his eyes. Helen's sad, genuine tone made him want to scream at her.

"Sorry I screwed up a possible romance," he said with great effort to cover his sarcasm.

"Your deeds and efforts to assist Yitzak and me in ending the Daniels affair are not forgotten, even at the personal cost. There are many more fish in the sea."

"Thank God for that," Glenn said as he looked down the long hill that crossed over about four busy streets. His destination was at the very bottom. Rue University would be the first street. He remembered a cafe that was right there. He looked further down and was glad to see that there were no major traffic jams. He moved his hand from his cheek and adjusted his clothes and retied his sneakers.

"So, how's the traffic?"

"It's surprisingly moving much better now. If I were you, I would move out. I will get there faster than anticipated. John and another colleague are also on the way and will probably get there at about the same time."

Glenn was appreciative that Helen was now all business. The sooner he left Montreal behind the better. While he liked the people and the city, he was especially happy that his pale skin did not really stand out. He was thinking about all the things he would miss about the place when he had a sick, palpable feeling that he was being watched. He walked slowly at first and placed his fake book bag across his body in case a sprint was required. He felt perspiration forming on the back of his neck as he tried desperately to pick up speed without giving any indication of fear and trepidation.

"Hey! Watch it! What's your problem?" (in French) he heard from behind. It was a loud, angry male voice and it was maybe a half a block from him. Little was lost in translation. He turned, as did a couple of other people who heard the same commotion. He took immediate note of two women wearing sunglasses who were now looking right at him. He froze as did they. Ana Ramsey, the one who gave him the scar back in Spain, looked very happy. The taller woman, the one he had seen in the UK months ago, looked really pissed. Both were dressed professionally but it was obvious they were ready for action – their blazers were perfectly tailored to obscure the presence of firearms he was sure they were both sporting. Glenn suddenly remembered that the taller woman - pale skin, blonde hair, and dark red lipstick visible from a distance - was the one he gave the finger to after Helen had rammed their car. With Daniels dead and Burns let free, he had hoped then as he did now to be free of the past. Like a shot, Glenn turned and ran for his life. More yells from angry pedestrians could be heard getting louder behind him.

"They spotted me, Helen! Make it quick!"

"I'll be there in less than two minutes."

"I'll be coming in hot! Your girlfriend is fast," he blurted out. He was running at full tilt. He felt his lungs filling and expelling air so fast his ribs began to hurt. He was successful at ducking and weaving around and through people on the sidewalks but he had to make a break for the middle of the street to not only move faster but to get to his destination. Rue University was well behind him and he had just narrowly escaped being hit crossing over Rue Aylmer. By now he was running in the middle of the street and Rue Durocher was fast approaching.

"Helen!?"

"I am turning onto Ave. du Parc now. John is ahead of me," she reported.

Glenn heard a number of screeching brakes behind him on Rue Durocher as he flew down Rue Hutchison, the last street before he turned left toward Cinema du Parc. He hoped that his race across the traffic might slow his adversaries down. He turned briefly and caught the taller woman far too close for his liking. He was beginning to feel gassed out and his legs were hurting at the top speed at which he had been moving. But with Ave. du Parc sign just ahead, he felt a burst of adrenalin kick in and he sped up as he headed into oncoming traffic. His arms and legs were pumping faster than he had ever remembered. Dodging moving cars, he passed a number of angry motorists. One black car barely missed him and seemed to brake hard after he passed. Another red car with orange flames on the backside and door skidded to a stop with the passenger side door flying open. Glenn hit the red car to stop his momentum and to catch his breath.

"Get in!" he heard Helen yell from inside.

Glenn caught his breath and moved to the open door. His legs felt like lead and his breathing was now ragged. He looked up the street and saw John and another man already out of their car and blocking the taller, pale-skinned woman's path, as if they were law enforcement. Glenn looked on in complete surprise when the woman had not slowed down at all but instead leaped sideways with her whole body hitting both men full force to the ground. It was as if a lightning bolt had struck the men down.

"Holy shit!"

Glenn was so surprised at the human crash that it took him a second to readjust his vision from the bodies on the ground to the second woman who was running full speed with a gun in each hand.

"Halt!" he heard the woman shout.

"Jeffery! Get in the car!"

Glenn moved quickly into the car just as bullets flew by him and glass, mirrors and metal shattered and cracked all around him. With the sole exception of a very sharp sting erupting in his upper arm, Glenn was thrilled to be in the car and moving relatively unscathed. He was genuinely amazed that Ramsey's aim was dead on the car even though she was running and several feet away when she started shooting. As the car pulled away and the civilians' screams and shots receded, there were still shots hitting the back of the car which shattered the rear window. They both ducked in their seats as yet another stray bullet hit the rearview mirror.

"Jesus Christ! How you liking her now?"

"She is exciting!" Helen said as she deftly maneuvered the car in and out of moving traffic just in case Ramsey and Dillon had confiscated a pursuit vehicle. He was sure they would try.

"You do have a *je ne sais quoi* with these two women," she added.

"And you must have a death wish to find her exciting."

Glenn smiled and tried to catch his breath. The car was moving quickly but was near the speed limit. It took a moment for him to speak again. His throat was dry and he felt very tired. He moved his left arm and when he did, it hurt.

"Ah, hell. Probably a shard of glass," he said as he looked at the blasted-out rear window for any indication of pursuit. As he turned his focus forward, he caught a look from Helen that appeared surprised at first but then she smiled. While still driving, she leaned over to the glove compartment, opened it and moved things around until she found a first aid kit. Her proximity and touch were warm and the strong smell of vanilla bean was refreshing after his dead run. She plopped the first aid kit on his lap and continued driving. He looked at it and then looked at her for some idea of what her problem was or where she might be hit.

"Helen? Where are you hit? I bet it's just got some glass," he said. As he attempted to open the kit, he noticed his arm really seemed to hurt whenever he moved it.

"You are quite adorable, Jeffery. I am not hit," she said with a smile. "Once again, I believe your shorter, dark nemesis will leave another scar. Not as clean, not as visible as the first but definitively a well-shaped one. Maybe the shape of a heart?"

Glenn let a sigh out as he realized that the kit was for him for sure. He looked at his upper arm and there was a bleeding gash that cut through his light jacket and shirt. No artery but definitively a direct hit. It really began to feel like hell and it looked as if the bullet passed right through.

"Please, Jeffery. Try not to bleed in this car. This is John's car and he will be angry enough at being taken down by one of your girlfriends and his vehicle being shot up. While the body work is doable, the upholstery is Italian leather and blood will be difficult to get out."

"Hunted, chased, and shot at. And I better not get blood on the seat," he muttered as he pulled gauze out and applied pressure.

"Yes. While we are on the subject of being hunted and it is evident that my requests to leave you alone have gone unheeded by Lieutenant Andersen and his associates, I suggest we relocate you to a place where it should be impossible for an American business such as Allied Federation International to send its agents," Helen said.

Still focused on his aching arm, Glenn asked what he thought would be a near impossible question to answer.

"And where might that be? I don't think North Korea, Russia or even China are viable options for the Mossad to relocate an asset such as myself."

"Agreed," she said.

Despite the wind traveling through the broken windows and some rattling in the car's frame, Glenn decided to continue with his line of questioning.

"Okay, Helen. I give up. Where were you thinking?"

"Cuba."

Glenn looked at her askance at first. As he thought about it, he found that her logic and reason might have a valid point. While the sun did not really appeal to him, the fact that Ramsey and everyone would be greatly hindered from skipping over to Cuba was intriguing. He remained silent as she listed the pros and cons.

"What do you think?" Helen asked.

"I think it has promise," he answered. Another minute of silence before Helen spoke again.

"Jeffery? I am serious. Do not get blood on the upholstery. John will get very angry."

Glenn looked at his wound and realized he needed more gauze and bandages to keep his blood from spilling over.

"Ah yes. Sorry," he said. Salt air, fresh bread and sugar cane and maybe even a real Cuban cigar paraded across his inner eye.

"Yeah."

"Pardon?" Helen asked.

"Cuba does sound like a great idea."

"Yes. It does. Lots of dark women there. I might even visit."

Glenn closed his eyes at both the thought of standing out as a "snowflake" and the thought of Helen hanging out to get lucky.

"Are you alright? Are you in shock?"

"Yes, Helen, but not from the gunshot," he replied. He looked out the window as he thought more about Cuba.

Eagle: Paris, France, EU
May 2nd – 3:00 PM

"Alone, alone, all, all alone,
Alone on a wide wide sea!
And never a saint took pity on
My soul in agony."

> *The Rime of the Ancient Mariner, Part IV,* Samuel Taylor Coleridge

ALICA WISE LOOKED MOMENTARILY at the young couples walking hand-in-hand down the Parisian street not far from Carr's Cellar Bar adjacent to the posh Le Meurice Hotel. The bar still had some patrons but since it was well after lunch, there were fewer people for sure. For a weekday, the street was not jammed with pedestrians since everyone was at work or in the park enjoying the gorgeous May day. Alica made sure she blended in with the other business people; she had very fashionable shoes, a short dress with a matching waist-length blazer and blouse. While it was warm, her blazer effectively concealed her small handgun with silencer, serrated switch blade on her right hip and her holstered collapsible baton under her right arm opposite her holstered gun. She shifted her gaze back to Jillian Davis whom she spotted hours ago. It was evident she was tracking someone. To her great surprise, she swore she caught view of Alexander Burns. It was fleeting but she was sure. She was positive Davis was alone and had spent hours watching, following and being patient. She had changed her sunglasses twice and her scarf three times. She could see that Davis was talking to someone, animated at times, and she was sure it was her boyfriend based on the way she was acting. It took her a great deal of time to find Davis and eventually Martin, the man she hated almost as much as Burns.

Based on the pattern Davis had traversed so far, Alica was able to predict her next move and cut several blocks ahead of her to wait, see if Burns was indeed ahead of her, let her pass, and then shoot her in the back of the head twice. A swift immediate kill in broad daylight and then she would be off to Germany to see if she could find Burns's alleged girlfriend. More young couples passed. She found herself getting angry. She usually was calm and sedate when she was close to a kill.

"Maybe it's all these fucking happy people," she muttered to herself. She turned to look into a window as if she were shopping. She took in her petite image and smiled. She had gotten looks from mostly men but she was focused on her mission. She looked down the street and saw Davis, still talking on her wireless earphone looking across the street. Alica smiled.

"No, Jillian. You'll pass right by me like so many others. You'll look at me and it won't register who I am at all. My hair is red and short. Very French. And my clothes are very professional, administrative-assistant-like, right down to these beautiful shoes and absolutely perfectly sheer pantyhose. Nope. Just walk on by. I'm a ghost," Alica said as she counted the narrowing steps between her and Davis. She turned to look back at the window, and verified that the store was right next to an alleyway. It was a large alleyway but it created a natural escape route. Davis would pass her, cross the street and before she was back on the other sidewalk, there would be two bullets in her head and Alica would be down the alley with the few tourists jumping out of her way. Alica counted to herself the timing when Davis might pass. She looked down at her leg as if she were looking for a run in her hose. There was a group of young women ahead of her and it looked as if there was an older couple well behind her. There was more foot traffic across the street and the road did seem a bit more busy than she would like.

"Can't plan everything."

She casually unholstered her small semiautomatic handgun and took out her silencer with the other. Her blazer and body hid them from Davis's view while she waited patiently for the group of women to pass. She had her back turned to them as if she were just waiting for someone on the street corner. As she waited, she saw an adorable buff cockapoo sitting perfectly on its hind legs on a bench looking at her. The cute creature was leashed to the bench handrail and looked serene. The clear brown eyes, perfectly clean, groomed fur and two pink bows tied to a very well-appointed collar made Alica smile.

"Now that's the way all dogs should be treated. Someone really loves you, don't they?" she said to the dog. The women passed her. One looked at her as if she might ask her something but looked away to talk to her companions. Another woman went to pet the dog, but the dog growled and then snapped at the woman's attempt to pet her. The women yelped in unison and picked up their pace to put distance between them and the tied-up pet.

"Good dog. You told her not to touch you. Fucking people," she said quietly. Alica waited and kept her back to Davis to let her pass. She had successfully affixed the silencer to her handgun. She heard Davis's voice. It was clear she was listening to someone. Alica felt her heart finally pound a bit faster. She was not feeling her joyful sense of anticipation of payback. She didn't know why.

"All right, already. As long as I get my game room and the insulation between our bedrooms, I'll be more than happy."

Davis was still talking as she passed her. Alica let her get eight feet ahead of her before she started moving herself. She kept both hands on her gun and toward the buildings, out of view from the street. Davis was just stepping off the curb as Alica closed the gap. She looked briefly down the alley and saw people walking in the opposite direction. Her heart jumped at the good fortune, she shifted her look back to Davis and turned to see the cockapoo still sitting but its small tail was wagging furiously and her eyes looked so excited. Alica smiled at how happy the dog looked at her.

Such a cute thing!

A bright light of orange, yellow and red flashed several stories above her across the street. It stole her attention. She looked back and saw the dog turn quickly to see the light just as the explosion erupted across the street. Shattered glass, metal and wood rained down to the ground as screams started in earnest. Alica immediately looked back at Davis but her attention was diverted by a strong grip on her gun hand and a very strong crack on her neck, just below the base of her skull. Her eyes immediately dimmed and she felt her legs give way. Her arms went limp and she felt air being pressed out of her stomach as if she were being hoisted by the waist from behind. She felt completely disoriented at first as she fought to remain conscious and feel for her gun. Without warning, she felt her whole body being violently pushed face first into a brick wall.

"Shit..." she muttered as she felt the front and back of her head instantly throb in pain. She was vaguely aware of her body being thoroughly and roughly searched. Her mind spun, wondering if it was all a trap and if law enforcement was all over her. But the speed and violence with which it all happened as well as the efficiency and ruthlessness led her to believe it wasn't the police or INTERPOL. Finally, she got feeling in her feet and tried to use her hands to push away from the wall. As she did so, she felt herself being whipped around in place so that her legs crossed, her spine wrenched and her butt, back and skull came in solid contact with the brick wall. Her eyes opened wide as the shooting pain rippled through her entire body. Her vision caught her own serrated knife plunging deep into her left shoulder.

"What...what the hell..."

Still reeling from the shock of a knife penetrating one shoulder, she next caught sight of her own gun pointed inches away from her other shoulder. Without any warning, it discharged twice. The silencer was loud at that short range. The pain from the shots was matched only by the violent removal of the knife that had stabbed her. She thought she heard her knife fall to the ground but her right arm was forcefully extended at the shoulder and turned over and she suddenly felt a sharp crack right across the two bones in her forearm.

There was silence for just a second, and then she felt herself suck in air as if she had stopped breathing throughout the entire assault. She sensed that she was sliding down to the ground but then she felt both her feet pulled out from under her. The crash to the ground jolted her. She could only hear herself trying to breathe, gasping for air. A siren sounded and she felt her face being slapped and heard someone talking to her. It was not a gentle slap but a determined one meant to wake her up. Alica moved her head up slowly but then felt someone pull it up and let it hit the wall again.

"Wake up, Alica Wise," the female voice said. The voice was firm, clear and exacting. It took every bit of strength to block out the pain and keep from weeping in pain. She struggled to look the woman in the eyes. She looked familiar but her own eyes were cloudy with tears, sweat and blood and the only thing she could be sure of was that the woman was strong, had long black hair, pale white skin and piercing blue eyes.

"Next time I see you, you won't see me, and you will be dead," the woman said without much emotion. Alica was still struggling to breathe as she watched the woman stand up in a long, dark coat that seemed to billow as she stood above her. She raised her metal baton above Alica and brought it crashing down onto her right ankle. The pain from the strike ran through her as if it were live current running through her whole body which now felt like a live wire after being shot, stabbed, pounded, beaten and broken. She never heard the heavy metal baton drop to the ground but she watched it clatter around and roll towards her. Alica slowly sunk from a seated position against the wall down to the ground. She focused on breathing as she watched the woman, definitely tall and athletic in her long coat that made her look dark as death but graceful as a swan. When the woman reached the entrance to the alleyway, she casually dropped the weapon's silencer and discharged the entire clip into the air before tossing the weapon at her. Alica took a moment to try to move something she thought wasn't in pain. The assault might have taken ninety seconds at the most. Alica laid her head on the street and hoped either death or unconsciousness would take her away from the pain. She felt pebbles and dirt touch her cheek and her vision tunneled quickly as she felt as if she might be leaving her body.. As she faded, she saw the cute cockapoo that looked so happy to see her before the explosion and the assault. She felt the corners of her mouth weakly pull up at how the dog looked happy to see her. She had no idea how much time had passed. Distant sounds of sirens, yelling, strong voices barking orders could be heard. They were not clear at all but instead muffled as if she were just outside of reality. She felt someone gently touching her cheek, the only place on her body that didn't feel broken, crushed, stabbed or shot.

"You're going to be okay, Alica. The EMTs are here."

Alica tried to focus her eyes and was pretty sure she made out the voice and face of Jillian Davis. The voice was the only thing she could hear clearly.

She heard another voice outside her field of vision. It was that of another woman.

"She has no idea how lucky she is to be alive."

Alica faded again. The cute dog sitting at the bench wagging its tail made her happy.

"Cute....dog..." she thought she heard herself say quietly.

Kitty Hawks: Montreal, Quebec, Canada
May 2nd – 9:35 AM

"The many men, so beautiful!
And they all dead did lie:
And a thousand thousand slimy things
Lived on; and so did I."

> *The Rime of the Ancient Mariner, Part IV,* Samuel Taylor
> Coleridge

"SO YOU JUST HAD to start shooting both guns in a crowded street at Snowflake? You gotta funny way of keeping 'low key,'" Dillon said quietly to Ramsey. Even with the hustle and bustle of law enforcement agents from multiple agencies, crime scene units everywhere and scores of civilian onlookers gawking at them, it was apparent that Ramsey was still fuming from her missed opportunity.

"I wasn't the one who took out the French and Canadian Secret Service guys."

"They didn't identify themselves," Dillon said defensively.

"That's because you were already airborne when they raised their hands. And don't bullshit me – you took them both out to give me a clean line of fire," Ramsey said.

"Yes, Ana! With one gun! What the hell were you thinking, going all 'wild west' out there?"

"I was thinking of hitting our target!"

"With the hail of bullets that rained down on him, you'd think you'd something!"

"Hey, you two! Pipe down or you'll go into separate cars," one of two burly Canadian military police officers said.

Dillon turned quickly to make sure that Ramsey was not going to mouth off. Dillon's ribs were aching and Ramsey sported a black eye. Not from the tackle and pursuit but from the brawl they both had with the Canadian authorities that swooped in to contain the situation. Dillon's frosty gaze at Ramsey stopped her from saying something. By now, standing handcuffed to the cruiser's locked doors was getting old and tiring. Both women remained silent as they watched a portly middle-aged man who barely fit into a gray suit two sizes too small was talking to nearly everyone they had managed to hurt, injure, knock down and piss off. It was a lot of people. Right behind him was a female officer who was dressed in uniform but similar to him, it was too tight. While the man's attire did little to flatter his apple-shaped physique, her tight apparel enhanced her body. She trailed behind him with a pen and leather notepad. Ramsey nodded at the woman's shoes. Dillon followed the gaze. The woman's shoes were not Canadian police-issue for snow tracking or walking a beat but were very flattering with black spiked heels making the tall woman tower over her short, balding boss.

"Let me guess, Staff Superintendent Baker," Ramsey said.

"Yup. He looks worse than his picture for sure. It looks like she's bucking for promotion," Dillon said as she looked away. She hated that kind of stuff.

"It's such bullshit," Ramsey said. Dillon turned to observe her and saw Ramsey looking down the blocked street. With barriers everywhere and traffic at a standstill, Dillon saw two black SUVs that were stopped with two men standing outside them talking to the military police at the end of the street.

"Must be for us. Probably going to throw us in their federal pen," Dillon said.

"Not likely, you terrible women. Even as we speak, the Chief of Police and Mayor are fighting over which penitentiary you will find most unappealing," Staff Superintendent Baker said. His voice was high-pitched for such a portly man. He was flanked by the two men Dillon had taken out with a body blow and the attractive female officer. She stood taller than all of them. If she was supposed to be taking notes or transcribing, she wasn't doing it well.

"I suppose it's 'guilty until proven otherwise' here," Ramsey said.

"We have many prisons with women that I am sure you will find appealing," one of the men said.

"You talking from personal experience, *petite fille*?" Dillon blurted out.

"No, Dillon. He's that guy's bitch. When I kicked him in the balls, there was a petit penis there, I swear. Or it could have been his keys," Ramsey added. One of the men moved to hit Ramsey. Dillon stepped in to kick him in the shin. It took a few seconds for the other officers, two inspectors and three crime scene specialists to break them up. Even as they separated, Dillon could still hear Ramsey shooting off her mouth.

"Try that when I don't have handcuffs, bitch!"

Once there was some semblance of order, the Superintendent stepped back in with his assistant behind him. As he was about to make some kind of pronouncement, a very strong voice came from behind him. All turned to see two men approaching. The taller of the two - a well-dressed man sporting a very well made navy blue suit, sunglasses, and strong, chiseled features - was walking towards them. As he got closer, his dark features and tanned face seemed at odds with his stylish suit and the Russian flag pin prominently placed on his lapel. His companion who casually brought up the rear was a man with equally chiseled features, well-dressed and groomed, sporting expensive sunglasses. This man was very dark, suggesting some kind of Hispanic or African origin. His suit was a dark brown that matched his skin, highlighted by a gold wristwatch and earring. He was clearly genetically gifted with muscles or he worked out all the time. *Impressive.*

"What is the meaning of this intrusion? This is a crime scene and I am the Superintendent," Baker started.

"Yes, Superintendent Baker. I am aware of who you are and your position within the Canadian force. My name is Victor and I am from the Russian Embassy. This is my Cuban colleague, Carlos.

We have business with these two Americans with regard to national security," he said smoothly. While his English was very good, it had an Eastern European accent. As he spoke, he handed the Superintendent a small camera that appeared to be showing a video or image. Carlos handed two documents to the other French men Dillon and Ramsey had just fought.

"The documents you are reading require the immediate release of Christine Dillon and Ana Ramsey into our custody and care. Please notice it is signed by your Chief of Police," Carlos said. His accent clearly indicated a Cape Verdean, Dominican or possibly Cuban origin. While the men who were reading the documents blanched, the Superintendent's face turned multiple shades of red. His jaw slackened and then shut as he frantically tried to turn the video off while Victor stood impassively and watched his desperate attempts.

"How do you make it stop?"

"You do not, Superintendent Baker. And if they are not released immediately into my care, this will be on the Internet in about ten minutes," Victor said. He looked at his watch with its elegant leather band. Baker continued to push buttons and then hit the device. He managed to give out his orders before he tried to walk away.

"Let them go. Now! Right now!"

"Excellent, Superintendent. I will personally let the Mayor and the Chief of Police know how helpful you were."

Dillon turned to see that Ramsey was in just as much shock as she was. She observed that both men holding their own documents were noticeably angry. One crumpled his document, threw it to the ground and stormed off. Dillon felt strong hands on her roughly releasing her handcuffs. Every time she breathed, her ribs hurt. Ramsey moved in to ask Victor a question. Victor put his hand up to stop her as he continued looking at the Superintendent and the female officer who had grabbed the camera, looked at it, threw it to the ground and slapped the Superintendent so hard Dillon felt her mouth ache in sympathy. The woman stormed off with the portly little man dropping to the ground to find the camera and then getting up as quickly as he could to chase after her.

"If you are going to dip your pen into company ink, you should do it at a hotel. Never have your paramour dress in your wife's wedding dress and make love in your own bedroom. Wives do not care much for that," he said with some degree of reflection in his voice.

"You're speaking from personal experience?" Ramsey blurted out.

Can't you ever shut up?

"No. I am not married. Children from two different women and plenty of support, but not married. Too burdensome," Victor said.

"Too restrictive. Better to keep options open," Carlos added. He turned to speak to the officer who had babysat Dillon and Ramsey for the last half-hour.

"Officer Roberts? Would you be so kind as to collect and retrieve Ms. Dillon's and Ms. Ramsey's personal affects, including their array of weapons, please?" she heard Carlos ask. There was a slight delay in response at first but then the officer turned and went to do the newly assigned task. Carlos followed him.

"Not that I'm not appreciative of your intervention, but who are you again?" Dillon asked. She turned to see if Ramsey was listening but she was fixated on Carlos's backside.

"Hey, Ramsey? Focus up here."

"Just surveying the scene," Ramsey said.

"It is all true what I said, Ms. Dillon. I am attached to the Russian Embassy, and Carlos is an adjunct to the Cuban Government," Victor said calmly. He was now standing with his hands in his pockets with his suit jacket still buttoned. It was clear that he was not a typical civil servant.

"So do you and Carlos often show up when American women with guns need help?" Ramsey said. Dillon was glad she finally focused in on the conversation.

"No, not really. I was reviewing the usual boring nothings that happen about the office when I received a text from Dr. Volkov Volkonoff asking me to check on your progress in apprehending Mr.

Jeffery Glenn. I had assured him that two recruits and a blind man could make our intelligence useful in his capture. But then I was contacted by my Cuban colleague Carlos who witnessed what you Americans call a 'cluster.' Anyway, I needed to make good on my statements to Dr. Volkonoff. It would be bad to disappoint him."

Dillon stood silently as she reviewed all the information. *The Wolf.*

"So Volkonoff sent you here to make sure we were all right?" Ramsey asked.

"No, Ana. He made sure that *we* make sure you apprehend Mr. Snowflake, I believe," Carlos said. Ramsey looked him up and down with little effort to cover up the fact that she was sizing him up.

"What's up?" she said.

"Nothing. What's up with you?"

"Nothing."

Dillon rolled her eyes and turned to talk to Victor who was already recovering from his smile.

"Dr. Volkonoff is following the recommendations of his niece, Ms. Rachael Janeson, and of Mr. Alexander Burns. The doctor has faith that their recommendations are in the best interest of our national security, Russian and American. Whatever he says, we do for him, president, flag and country. But enough of this, ladies. We must go," Victor said. By now there were two Canadian officers handing back their weapons, cash, wallets and personal items. Dillon was impressed with her own lack of reaction to the mention of Janeson's and Burns's names. Ramsey had followed suit in keeping her reactions at bay and continued with the data gathering.

That's what I like about you, Ana. Still always working even when you're checking out someone's ass.

"So where are *we* going?"

"We are going to locate your Snowflake and give you yet another opportunity to bring him in," Carlos said as he followed Victor's wake. Both men were heading to the car as Dillon and Ramsey were still putting all their equipment away.

"Not to be a negative Nancy, but we lost him and he has a

forty-plus-minute lead," Dillon said.

With her armory put back together, she was walking just a little more slowly to accommodate her hurt ribs and aching hips and arms. As she walked, she followed Victor, catching a full view of his impressive backside.

"Hey? You got any makeup?" Ramsey asked quietly. She pointed at her black eye to indicate the reason for it.

"What? Does it look like I got a purse? Focus, Ana."

"Like you were on Victor's butt? Now, when did you break up with Kevin?" Ramsey whispered.

"Two months ago because I was helping you chase a ghost. And it's a break. Shut up," she whispered back.

She saw Ramsey give a sly smile.

"Fortunately for you, Carlos here has many contacts along the Canadian and American coast and I have a great deal of resources. One of our resources discovered that the Mossad plans to escort Mr. Glenn to a very difficult place for you to gain entry into without our help. They plan to go to Cuba."

"Son of a bitch! Snowflake!" Ramsey said.

"Yes. His handler, Helen, is a very cunning and devious one. I respect her work and would prefer to take Glenn without harm to her," Carlos said. Victor shot a look at him. While both wore sunglasses, it was easy to see that both knew volumes.

"*Vy nad ney?*" Victor asked

"*Mozhet byt', da. Mozhet byt'n net,*" Carlos responded in perfect Russian.

"*Prosto velikolepno,*" Victor said. He shook his head and continued walking.

Dillon caught Ramsey looking and could tell she picked up on the same interaction. By now they were beyond the barriers and in the streets where there were well-dressed security men and women surrounding two waiting luxury SUVs.

"So, on behalf of the Russian and Cuban governments, we would like to offer our services in assisting your efforts to bring an INTERPOL fugitive to justice," Victor said. Just as he finished, his smartphone rang. It sounded like it was some Russian ringtone.

"It will be an adventure. I actually hope he makes it to Cuba. It would be nice to feel the soil and sun again," Carlos said wistfully. Dillon was about to object and walk away from the SUVs when Carlos handed her his phone.

"It is for you, Ms. Dillon. It is Mr. Gilmore from the FBI in Boston. He seems very adamant to talk to you."

"Gilmore's on the line? What the hell?" Ramsey said.

Dillon was just as shocked as Ramsey. She took the phone and said "hello."

"Dillon? Wake the hell up! I got some serious shit going on in Paris with Davis and Cratty so I don't have time for a long story."

"Are they alright?" Dillon jumped in. Her thoughts quickly focused on how half her team was killed in Spain. Cindy Belben, Kelly Fitzgerald, and Molly Horowitz. Guilt pulled at her for not being there.

"They're fine, Dillon. I got to send Davis and Cratty some shit about Janeson. You need to contact Welch or Helms. They met *Wolf.* Green light to go with Carlos and Victor. Crystal?"

"Clear. We're green to go. Good luck."

"You too," she heard Gilmore say. Before she heard him sign off, she could hear him yelling something at Johnson. *Just like old times.*

"So are we staying or going with them?" Ramsey had been listening to her side of the discussion. Dillon handed Victor his phone. He plopped it in the breast pocket of his coat and stood with his hand in his pocket. Dillon took her time taking in the lay of the land before she responded to Ramsey's question.

"We're going with them."

Ramsey smiled as Victor nodded.

"Alright then, ladies. Carlos has an idea of where to start the hunt," Victor said as he held the SUV's rear passenger door open.

"Here we go," Ramsey said with zeal.

"Here we go," Dillon said.

Doves: Paris, France, EU
May 2nd – 3:35 PM

Water, water, everywhere,
And all the boards did shrink;
Water, water, every where,
Nor any drop to drink.

> *The Rime of the Ancient Mariner, Part II,* Samuel Taylor
> Coleridge

"WHAT THE HELL IS wrong with you, Burns?" Jillian Davis muttered. Without hesitation, she touched her necklace even though there was no real fear of it being lost for she had checked it ten minutes ago. She pulled her hand down and surveyed the mass of law enforcement, first responders and a sea of "do not cross" yellow tape taking up nearly an entire city block in the "City of Love." The explosion, limited damage to people but a spectacular display of pyrotechnics was classic Alexander Burns. The only difference was Alica Wise's beating. Every weapon on her person was used against her. While the old Burns from years ago would have simply shot her execution-style, this mauling of her with her own weapons seemed more of a deadly message. What the message was exactly, Davis was not sure. To her left and right was a series of French police talking to various people, possible witnesses. Right in front of her was a much smaller group of INTERPOL agents interviewing a few witnesses that might have actually seen something. The street was still littered with cars trapped from the debris from the apartment explosion just across the street. The smell of ash, extinguished fire, and car fumes filled the beautiful May day. Davis scanned the ground behind her to make sure all the evidence was still in place and that the crime scene team had the area secured before she joined Cratty on the other side of the street. Hints, clues and evidence abounded. If this was Burns, it was a classic case of flooding the area with information, misdirection and distraction to confuse and delay the enemy. The intel was everywhere and nowhere at the same time. Davis shook her head as a way of clearing her mind of Burns's subterfuge. She refocused her efforts to find her partner. It was easy to see that Denise Cratty was deep in discussion with three women and two INTERPOL agents. Davis chuckled to herself as she approached the scene. Davis had watched how rehab, home-making and falling in love had made Cratty more mature. Not that she wasn't mature to start, but her use of a cane while wearing very stylish clothes that bordered on New York/Paris fashion made her look both seductive and chic, mature and young: a thigh-high skirt with matching blazer and gold jewelry including an anklet.

"An anklet? Really? You are such a girly-girl. No wonder you had to ride in the car," she said to herself. And while Davis still preferred her own plain, functional attire, she found herself acting as Cratty's older sister - more often than not, it seemed, much to Cratty's chagrin. But even as she approached her in the midst of a lively discussion, Davis found herself yet impressed with another skill that Cratty had not shared with her, despite having been housemates. She slowed her pace down to listen carefully to make sure she was actually hearing what she thought she heard.

"*Also, sie war gross, mit einem schwarzen, wallenden Mantel, langem schwarzem Haar, blasser Haut und strahlenden Augen?*" Cratty said in excellent German.

"*Ja, sie war gross aber sehr kräftig gebaut,*" the redhead said.

"*Ja! Sehr eindrucksvoll! Aber sie hat dann die Pistole geschossen und wir sind weggelaufen,*" the brunette added.

"*Et ça, c'est quand tu es retournée à la police près de l'explosion,*" the INTERPOL agent said. It looked as if he was asking questions while his partner was writing everything down. Cratty nodded and turned to the German women and asked what

Davis surmised was the same question.

You got to be kidding me. She knows German? No way!

"*Ja, wir haben ihm alles erzählt aber als wir hier angekommen sind war sie bereits weg und dann haben wir jene arme junge Frau gefunden*". Cratty nodded as if she understood and repeated something in French. The French INTERPOL agent nodded and spoke directly to Cratty in French.

Is that French? What the hell? Davis stood behind her quietly with her arms folded.

Cratty listened intently as she leaned on her cane. Beige silk suit, hem too high, shoes that were classic but far from functional, tasteful jewelry and a red, beige and black scarf around her neck that pulled it all together. With the addition of her longer blonde hair, tanned skin and stylish sunglasses, Cratty looked more like a petite fashion model than a seasoned private military contractor.

And she also knows two foreign languages to act as an interpreter? Of course. Cooks superbly, decorates well, dresses exquisitely, and fluent in two languages. There are times I wish I was gay. I wonder if Martin speaks a different language? I should ask more questions.

"*Merci, Madame* Cratty. *Transmettez nos amitiés à Madame Ramsey et à Madame Dillon,*" the officer said as the other agent rounded up the three women. Before they were carted off, one woman broke away and said something to Cratty as she handed her a note.

"*Wir werden um neun Uhr im Cafe am Dachgeschoss des Hotels ,,Le Meurice" sein. Komm und schliess dich uns an!*" the redhead said with a smile and a wave.

"*Ich gehe mit jemandem aus, aber danke für die Einladung.*"

"*Wir auch. Bringen Sie sie mit. Wenn Sie in Hamburg sind, bringen Sie Ihre Freundin mit,*" the brunette added. The other two women giggled as Cratty smiled and said something in a low tone. One of the INTERPOL agents who watched the entire interaction smiled as the other handed him some cash. As the group disbanded, Davis watched Cratty slip the small card into her blouse and was clearly surprised to see that she had been behind her all this time.

"Jesus, Davis. I'm going to have to put a bell on you. What did you find out?"

"What that hell was that about?" Davis said. It came out more forcefully than she had expected.

Davis was surprised that Cratty blushed and it was clear she chose her words carefully.

"Linda and I like meeting new people. And Linda really likes redheads. Don't be judgmental, Davis. I thought we were beyond that?"

It took a minute for Davis to see that she had really misunderstood Cratty.

"I'm not talking about the women, Denise. I'm used to that, for God's sake. I'm talking about you knowing French and German. Geez, Denise, kind of defensive about the girl thing, huh?"

"Oh. I just thought you were having a change of heart about the renovations, you wanting extra insulation between the walls," Cratty said.

Davis rolled her eyes and started to walk back to the alleyway as her phone vibrated. She pulled it out, thankful to have something to keep her hands from gripping her necklace.

"I want a game room for me, Martin and everyone to hang out in, and I want to be able to sleep at night when you and Linda are entertaining."

"I never complain about you and Martin." Even though Cratty needed a cane, Davis never slowed down for her to keep up. Somehow Cratty did keep up, if not a foot or so behind her. Davis privately liked that arrangement.

"That's because it's just the two of us and we're quiet when we do our thing. You and Linda, and the *others* get a bit too into it. It's a volume and number thing, not *just* an enthusiasm thing. I'm just talking about being able to sleep," Davis said. She was glad that caller identification said "Gilmore." She took the call without hesitation in the hopes that Cratty would stop talking about her noisemaking.

"What'd you get from INTERPOL's surveillance?"

"Plenty and it's not pretty. Find a private spot for you and Cratty to listen in on speakerphone. I'm sending Cratty the footage we got from the cafe and across the street."

"Why don't you just send it to me? I can run the video and speakerphone."

"Because you're technologically deficient and Cratty has an updated smartphone with high definition. She's part of the 21st century," he answered. Davis frowned and could already see that Cratty was getting footage. It took a minute to find a quieter part of the street that had fewer people.

"Go" Davis said. She and Cratty huddled close with Cratty's large smartphone coming alive with crystal-clear black and white footage and Gilmore's voice narrating the action.

"So, Davis? Today I would buy a lottery ticket. Watch the woman who you just passed by the store window near the street."

Davis watched herself on the small screen and felt her heart speed up and anger boil in her stomach. She remembered seeing some woman, but she didn't connect it with Wise.

"Son of a bitch..." Cratty muttered.

Just as she moves out of camera view to the street, the image of Wise moving quickly behind her with her gun down by her side and ready to point and shoot was as clear as day. Wise looks down the alleyway, then turns to see a dog sitting on a bench, and suddenly a bright flash of the explosion. Before the light from the blast subsides, a tall woman in a long black coat swiftly appears behind her, simultaneously grasps Wise's gun hand and delivers a full hammer fist strike to the back of her head.

"Shit! No way!"

"Yup. We got it all wrong. It wasn't Burns," Gilmore said.

"I hate it when I'm right," she heard Johnson say in the background.

As Wise drops, the dark woman lifts her from behind with one arm while still manhandling Wise's weak gun hand. The next view was from the cafe but its depth of field and low lighting made it very difficult to see what was happening. The dark, blurred images hinted at Wise being hurled face first against the wall, frisked, and then there was some kind of discussion involving hitting and other swift movement. The sudden movements revealed the attacker's speed and efficiency. Davis and Cratty had to slow the video down to analyze what they thought were strikes but they still couldn't confirm the weapon. With her victim clearly helpless and kicked to the ground, the attacker squatted to say something, broke the victim's ankle with a baton and walked away. The transition from blurry, dark, jolting images to clearer, more defined video was startling. The next shot was from the street where the woman discharges the handgun, throws it back in the alley, and pulls her dark wig off to reveal short blonde hair. She turns her dark coat inside out, changing it from black to canary yellow in seconds, and places a set of sunglasses on her face to cover her eyes. Previously, she was thoroughly cloaked, her dress is full-length and blood red while her blouse is as canary yellow as her coat. The rapid transformation before her eyes was drastic as it was sudden. Again, Cratty slowed the image down to reveal the woman's very athletic body with a thin waist. Next the woman untied the dog's leash, gave her a quick pat and walked away as if she had just drunk a cup of coffee and was finishing the dog's walk.

"From dark assailant to blonde, chic, well-tailored dog owner. Time index from beginning to the end of the attack – eighty-one seconds. I've never seen Janeson in action and I'm not sure I like what I see. And she's a blonde now," Gilmore said. His tone was sullen, low and tired.

"You think you know someone," Cratty said aloud.

"Why the sudden change, and in plain view?" Gilmore asked.

"I bet she wanted us to immediately spot her and figure it was her but then let us know that she had literally changed, right in front of us," Cratty answered.

"Pretty symbolic and ballsy at the same time. I really didn't think this would happen."

"Nope. We knew it would happen," Davis said as she knit her

eyebrows.

Cratty looked at her askance but seemed to get what Davis was saying.

"Okay, Davis. Care to enlighten us?" Gilmore asked.

Instead of Davis, Cratty answered.

"Janeson didn't kill Wise. She beat the shit out of her to make it clear that if anything happens to Burns, she'll be dead before she knows it. This was Wise's warning. Pretty clear from a girl's perspective."

"And the changing of her appearance?"

"Cratty's right. She's letting us know that she shed her identity for something new. Maybe she really is a swan," Davis said. Her hand was firmly attached to her necklace. Her grip had tightened during the time she had watched the video.

"Gives a whole new meaning to 'stay away from my boyfriend.' It was your lucky day to be the one following Burns," Gilmore chimed in.

"*Trying* to follow Burns," Cratty corrected. "He ducked you a half hour ago."

Davis looked at Cratty and frowned.

"Not everyone gets to ride in a comfortable car looking at the sites when doing surveillance. I didn't see you following him."

"I've got some issues, Jillian!" Cratty shot back as she turned off her smartphone and gave Davis space to see her with the cane.

"Oh, God. You're pulling the disabilities card?"

"No! I'm telling you it's very hard to blend when you have a cane."

"Oh, you blend in here with your clothes and your fancy language," Davis said. She let her hand drop from her necklace.

"We're in France, Jillian. They're classy here. We're not at a boot camp!"

"Okay, ladies. It was nice talking to you. Johnson and I got some work to do – you know: protecting the world from terrorism. You remember that, don't you?" Gilmore said.

"Shut up, Gilmore," Davis and Cratty said at the same time.

"Hey, Johnson? Did you hear that? Davis and Cratty agreed on something! Break out the beer and..." Davis closed the line with zeal. Cratty nodded in approval. Both walked back to the alley where the crime scene unit was still working. The activity on the street was still active while they both stood quietly.

"So, Janeson has transformed," Davis said.

"And in the process saved your life," Cratty added.

"And immobilized and captured a very dangerous fugitive who killed a correction officer and her husband."

"Well, the proof is circumstantial."

"A guard under investigation for sexually harassing the convicts, who just so happened to be Wise's guard, and then she and her husband are brutally killed, but the cat is well taken care of? Well-fed and hydrated for days," Davis said.

"Oh, I'm sure she did it. But unless we get some DNA or a live witness, we'll only have very strong circumstantial shit," Cratty said.

"Yup."

"I'm not sure Burns helped her," Cratty said.

"Yup. He would have immobilized Wise. He wouldn't have let Janeson brutalize her. It was resourced and planned out well. She set everything to go. That meant she knew we would be here and that Wise would make her move on Burns. And when I showed up, that was her opportunity. So, if it's not Burns that's helping her..." Davis started.

"It's her uncle, the *Wolf.* It's a family thing. It's personal," Cratty said.

Both women stood quietly looking over a large crime scene. Davis was sure there would be no useful evidence, leads or hints to be found in the area.

"Not good. Not good at all. You were right about what you said about Wise," Davis said.

"I say a lot of things. What did I say about her?" Cratty looked at Davis as if it might remind her.

"She has no idea how lucky she is to be alive."

Falcon: Paris, France, EU
May 2nd – 5:10 PM

"Day after day, day after day,
We stuck, nor breath nor motion;
As idle as a painted ship
Upon a painted ocean."

> *The Rime of the Ancient Mariner, Part II,* Samuel Taylor
> Coleridge

"WILL THAT BE ALL, MONSIEUR?"

Alexander Burns looked up from his leather notebook. The French waitress was older than most, sensual and well put together. She was clearly the head of the small cafe that served the working poor. Having a guest like him must have been a treat based on her surprise when he arrived. Once she found out he spoke American English, she had insisted on his speaking in it rather than in French. She was clear she wanted to practice the foreign language. Even though big tips for services were frowned upon in the EU, that didn't stop Americans from giving them out when they felt taken care of by English-speaking servers. To the cafe's credit, the food, coffee and service were excellent.

"Yes. It was all very good, thank you," he replied. He moved his smartphone, small Wi-Fi television, and first responder scanner. To the casual observer, he must have looked like he was a journalist with a lot of high-tech gadgets to get him through. As she cleared all of the dishes, Burns noticed that the two young mothers with their sleeping infants were smiling at him again. Their young waitress had given them extra coffee, smaller containers of milk, and rolls. He was impressed that they were looking for extra money for the bill to give her for her kindness. She waved it off and walked away and then gave Burns's waitress their bill. She had looked at it and crossed something off and put it in her apron just before she came to collect his dishes.

He smiled back at the women and went back to his writing. It had only been a few months since he started journaling. A process of clearing your thoughts and organizing feelings, a technique David Caulfield had recommended years ago. "It engages the frontal lobe in organizing thoughts and feelings. Makes you more pro-social. An amazing thing," he had said often. The hardest part was learning to write script so the thoughts could flow faster, and then came the process of thinking about what to write. The weird part was that he caught on pretty fast and he found he liked the writing part. He even re-read it later which gave him more insights. He took a moment to see what he had already put down.

It's unusual for me to play such a small role in such an elaborate operation. I walked around for a couple of hours and that was it. I must be getting comfortable letting people do their thing and following their lead. It also helps that Rachael and her uncle really do know what they're doing. Not their first day on the job. It was something to see Davis and Cratty in the background of a local news report here. Even in the distant background they looked like they were arguing. I concur with Rachael's assessment that they are long-lost sisters. Very similar to Emma and Rosemarie. I'm glad that Rachael's uncle had a chance to meet Helms and Welch. As I suspected, he liked them both even thought he didn't want to admit it. After years of hearing the Wolf's name bantered about, it's strange to be connected to him somehow. Stranger that Rachael is related to him. That really had to piss off the NSA and FBI. So much for screening. She's really different from Samantha but her dedication to life is the same. In an odd way, I think Samantha would have really liked her. She wouldn't have understood her but she would have liked her. Becky seems to like her very much. Speaking of which, David, I'll have to talk to her about getting back on her medication.

Even though the thing with Panelli went alright, she sounds depressed as hell. I think she already knows what she has to do. I just have to mention it again. If Samantha was here, Becky would double her dose to get her off her back. You got to love her for that. Well, I got to run now. I have to get to Paris Gare du Nord if I'm going to catch the rail to Hamburg. After spending so much time at the Louvre, I think it's time to catch the "Sturm und Drang" movement at its source. The Kunsthalle Hamburg Museum holds the original Friedrich's Wanderer Above the Sea of Fog. *I'm this close and I have to see it for myself. You'd love it.*

Burns smiled at the thought of David appreciating such a piece of work. He had no idea at the time that the oil on canvas portrait was a favorite of Rachael's until he had a chance to talk to her for hours as he waited to be captured by Daniels. So many things he learned back then. And then there was the drug-induced state during which he saw everyone in his life who had died. It was crazy but he put it all in the journal as well. The more he wrote the better he felt. He scanned the area to see if his four shadows were still in place. Two men and a pair of women. The challenge was having Davis follow him and then ditching her but keeping his other tails on him. Their approach to surveillance was old-school. Effective but once identified, it was predictable. The Mossad had their way while the Americans had their own. These shadows were traditionally Russian. Not Soviet-era but not long after. They had been on this for a full month since the operation launched. *And here I thought I was being idle.*

"Thank you very much for coming to our cafe," the waitress said. "Where are you off to now?"

"Vienna, Austria. I've always wanted to visit the Kunsthalle Wien Museum," Burns said. After so many years of being an anti-terrorist specialist, giving his true destination was difficult to do. He chuckled at how quickly the lie came out. He put down the exact amount of change needed for the bill and then gave her a large tip.

"I hear they have a wonderful cafe in the museum," she said.

"Not as well-served and well-maintained as here, I'm sure. I'll be back to let you know," Burns said as he pulled all his stuff into his backpack.

"You are too kind," the server said. She stopped for a moment, baffled by the significantly larger amount of money he gave for the small bill.

"Give the cafe the coins and cash below. The euros on top are for you, and don't argue or I will not return," he said. At first the waitress was shocked at what he said and then surprised at the sheer amount of the tip. With some hesitation and then zeal, she took the euros and put it in her bra.

"You are very kind and generous, Monsieur," she said. Her face barely contained her gratitude. He was sure he just paid her a month's wages.

"I've been working on the generosity part for a year."

"Then I am very happy to assist in that. *Merci beaucoup!*"

"Oh and *Mlle*? Is that the two mothers' bill in your apron?" Burns asked.

The waitress looked startled at first, more likely thinking of what she would spend her newfound money on. She took a moment to regroup and pulled out their bill. Without a further word, Burns took it from her, read it, paid it in the exact amount as well, and gave his waitress a tip to give to their server. The woman's eyes were as wide as saucers. This was far from a usual event.

"You will make sure their server gets her tip, *s'il vous plaît?*"

"I most certainly will! *Merci encore!*"

Burns smiled and walked in the opposite direction of the other women and waitress. He was about a half a block away when he heard the cries of joy from a woman he was sure was the other waitress. Burns kept going without looking back. Once across, he dropped to one knee and re-tied his shoe. It was evident that the male surveillance team was on the move and the female team nowhere in sight. If all went accordingly, they would be at his next predicted sites. He stood back and continued his march. After a few more minutes, he checked his watch and pulled out his smartphone to find the schedules for the overnight train. The wallpaper was of

Rachael looking out over a mountain range while Roxie stared back at him. It always made him smile. He had time to actually stroll. *Yup. I'm pretty idle these days.* All of these things were new to him. He re-read an earlier text from Rachael:

It is a better May 2nd. Ms. Regina and Mr. Angelo Panelli are back in custody, as is Alica Wise in the hands of INTERPOL. Ms. Ana Ramsey and Ms. Christine Dillon are working with the Cubans and my uncle to find and capture Mr. Jeffery Glenn, and Ms. Jillian T. Davis lives to fight with Ms. Denise Cratty another day. RJ.

Burns continued to appreciate her sense of humor. While he had thought he had sent a witty response earlier, he was wondering if there was still more to add when another text came in. He paused at the ID for only a moment before he opened it up.

My niece's thirty-sixth birthday is coming up on January 10th. Her parents and I would like for you to join us in Moscow starting on Christmas. I prefer you meet me a week prior so we can talk in person. Let me know what your plans are. Volkonoff.

"A man of many talents. I hope he got this number from Rachael," he said. He took a few minutes to think of a response. It came to him in seconds but he took his time to make sure that every word was not wasted.

Certainly. Five days out give me your location. Should I assume I am being watched?

Burns stopped in front of a jewelry shop. A necklace caught his eye. It was of fine gold with an elegant black swan pendant. He felt for his own necklace as he looked closely at it through the shop window. A text came in.

Yes. You were very kind to the waitresses and the mothers. All the rumors about you changing seem to be true. Your surveillance is only for your protection. You are very important to my niece. No offense.

Burns smiled.

None taken. Thank you. Burns.

Burns checked to see if the shop was still open. He was grateful it was though he was sure he would be the only customer. The place looked quiet.

Pozhaluysta. Volkonoff.

He closed down the smartphone and took another look at the necklace.

"That would make a nice birthday present."

He looked at the others around it and then stepped into the shop.

List of Characters

Alexander J. Burns – aka "**Falcon 5**." First seen in *Albatross,* Burns survives a helicopter crash while en route to a black-ops mission to kill the terrorist leader, Oman Sharif Sudani. Brain-injured, he finds treatment in the form of a former nurse, Samantha Littleton and Dr. David Caulfield. The treatment helps him regain his memory, and realizes he is a logistics field operative for the Foreign Intelligence Agency, FIA. In *Raven* and in *Eagle*, this knowledge and the FIA's deadly response resulted in the deaths of Samantha, his lover, and Dr. Caulfield, the two people he remembered as being close to him. In *Falcon,* Burns is drugged and transported ostensibly to be killed by Daniels. In his drug-induced state, much is learned about Burns, and many questions answered.

Eric I. Daniels – aka "**Eagle**." Mentioned in *Albatross,* first seen in *Raven*, and fully elaborated on in *Eagle,* he is the Chairman of the FIA, a privately held, clandestine intelligence agency that will work on behalf of the United States government when it aligns with its own interests and objectives. He is the one that assigns **Alica Wise** to find and kill Burns and employs the crime siblings **Regina and Angelo Panelli** who in turn recruit **Jeffery Glenn**, former FIA Manager, to kidnap Burns's family. Wise's attempts are thwarted by Jillian Davis while Burns's efforts to save Emma's sister **Rosemarie** prove successful. All of these characters are highlighted in *Eagle*.

Becky Littleton – aka "**Tiny**." Introduced in *Albatross* as Samantha's older foster sister as well as **Emma Littleton**'s primary caretaker after her brother, Tony, is killed by the mob. In *Raven*, her lethal skills grow exponentially, as does her role as mother, sister and wife. It is in *Eagle*, following the death of her husband, Dr.

Caulfield, that she is confronted with the caretaking of Emma's half sister, **Rosemarie**. As a result, Becky needs to come to terms in dealing with former South Boston mobster, **John Daniel Murphy**, the father of the man who killed her brother, Tony Littleton.

Steve Andersen – Lieutenant, North Reading Police Department, MA, is the first to interview the witness "Samuel Coleridge" in *Albatross*. Additionally, he was on the team of Army Intelligence at Guantanamo that connected the dots to locate Oman Sharif Sudani. He is also best friends with his colleague **Diane Welch** who grew up in the same South Boston neighborhood. His role expands as a key force trying to find out the truth at all costs with Diane Welch and Boston Regional FBI Director **John Helms**. He plays a prominent role throughout all the books.

John Helms – FBI Director, Boston Regional Office, he is the first to detect the diversions and covert plan in *Albatross,* as well as attempt a negotiation for peace with Burns in *Raven*. He was also **Diane Welch's** CO briefly in Afghanistan. At the end of *Falcon*, he retires from the FBI to work with Diane Welch at Allied Federation International, Inc.

Rachael Janeson – aka "**Black Swan.**" Specialist at the FBI Boston Regional Office in *Albatross*, she becomes lead specialist in *Raven* where she exposes a plot to thwart the FBI's attempt to bring Burns into custody. She is promoted to Deputy FBI Director in *Eagle* where she manages a rescue operation in Spain and a manhunt for **Jeffery Glenn** in Tangiers. At the end of *Eagle* and well into *Falcon*, her growing relationship with Alexander Burns draws the attention of the NSA when they open a thorough investigation. The results are startling and are finally explained by **Gilmore** and **Johnson**, her closest colleagues, after they uncover still more of her secret life.

Diane Welch – Commandant, Massachusetts State Troopers, first mentioned in *Albatross* as Steve Andersen's close friend. In *Raven*, we discover she was a Warrant Officer of a Marine Air Ground Task Force on a covert operation to stem the flow of arms from the Swat Valley, Pakistan. Betrayed by Thomas Webber, member of Daniels' FIA team in *Raven*, her role continues in *Eagle* with her in hot pursuit of Eric Daniels until his demise in *Falcon*. The President's head of Secret Services convinces her to become President & CEO of a major defense company, Allied Federation International, Inc. She pulls together her team that includes John Helms, Steve Andersen, Jillian Davis, Denise Cratty, Christine Dillon and Ana Ramsey.

Jillian T. Davis – aka **"Cougar."** First seen in *Albatross,* she is an off-duty manager of the FIA's Operations Center who is recruited to courier top-secret external hard drives to a secure location. In *Raven*, Davis leaves the FIA and teams up with the FBI to negotiate with Burns, while in *Eagle*, she is lead field specialist with Welch's former team, **Thomas "Nine" Williams** and **Daniel "Ice" Maddox**, to disrupt Daniels' plans and take down one of his key players. In *Eagle* and *Falcon*, her understanding of her nemesis, **Denise Cratty**, becomes clearer and an unlikely friendship blossoms.

Denise Cratty – Introduced in *Albatross,* she is the on-duty manager of the FIA's Operations Center when it is compromised. In *Raven*, Cratty is on probation in the new Operation Center where she is the unlikely peace-keeper in ending a dangerous standoff and then becomes lead agent on a VIP protection team in Spain. In *Eagle*, after tragedy strikes, she vows to bring her surviving team back to the US and find the people responsible. **Ana Ramsey** is the only other person of the protection team that made it back. **Christine Dillon** was reassigned back to the US before her former teammates were killed.

Jeffery Glenn – aka **"Snowflake."** Mentioned briefly at the end of *Albatross*, he is fleshed out in *Raven* as mild-mannered Operations

Center boss of Cratty and her team stationed in New York. In *Eagle*, after he is discharged from the FIA, he is paid for one last assignment that puts him on a path that will alter Cratty's and Burns's lives forever. In *Falcon*, he joins forces with the Mossad and the French and Italian Intelligence Agencies to find and terminate Eric I. Daniels. While he earns some positive points for this task and saves Burns, his past involvement in the ambush of **Denise Cratty**'s team and his escape from **Christine Dillon** and **Ana Ramsey** which put their safety at risk makes him their number one target to capture.

Emma Littleton – Introduced as a baby in *Albatross*, she is under the care of Becky Littleton and David Caulfield. She is introduced to her half-sister, **Rosemarie,** in *Eagle*. Their shared biological grandfather is the South Boston mob leader, **John David Murphy**.

Alica Wise – Introduced in *Eagle*, she is a former Foreign Intelligence Agent specialist recruited for the top-secret, deep-cover "Intimate Contact" branch. Still aligned with Daniels, she plans to carry out her orders no matter what. In *Eagle,* we gain more insight into her family and her fondness for animals over humans. By the time she is free in *Falcon*, she has settled some old scores but is still interested in killing two targets: **Jillian Davis** and **Alexander Burns**.

Christine Dillon & Ana Ramsey – First seen as part of Cratty's Operations Center team in *Raven*, they later become leaders in their own right in *Eagle*. They are close friends of Cratty and her fallen team members Cindy Belben, Kelly Fitzgerald and Molly Horowitz. In *Falcon*, they are teamed up by **Rachael Janeson** as backup to find Burns and, if possible, capture **Jeffery Glenn**.

John Daniel Murphy – Leader of organized crime in South Boston, he is the paternal grandfather of both Emma Littleton and her half-sister, Rosemarie Flores. His character is hinted at in *Albatross* and *Raven* as the father of the man who kills **Tony Littleton**. In *Falcon*,

Murphy and Becky Littleton join forces to protect the girls by using him as bait to lure out **Angelo Panelli** out from hiding.

Dr. Volkov Volkonoff – aka **"Wolf."** First mentioned in Falcon, his late appearance reflects the cloak of mystery that surrounds Rachael Janeson's maternal uncle. His involvement in the Russian intelligence community is well documented though unclear in details. With the sole exception of watching out for his niece, his motivations remain unknown.

About the Author

In addition to the award winning *Birds of Flight* series: *Albatross, Raven, Eagle* and *Falcon,* J.M. Erickson has written the critically acclaimed science fiction novellas *Future Prometheus I & II* series and *Intelligent Design: Revelations.* Erickson holds a BA in psychology and sociology from Boston College and master's degree in psychiatric social work from Simmons School of Social Work. He is senior instructor of psychology and counseling at Cambridge College, and senior therapist in a clinical group practice in the Merrimack Valley, Massachusetts, USA.

A Note from the Author

If you enjoyed this book please feel free to let your friends know about it. I would also appreciate it if you could leave a review. For more information on my other stories, please feel free to stop by my websites.

www.jmericksonindiewriter.com
www.jmericksonindiewriter.net